THE VOID

D.J. GOODMAN

SEVERED PRESS
HOBART TASMANIA

THE VOID

1

It was the single most disconcerting sight Vichna Lashke had ever seen in her life. On one side of the bridge's view screen she could see a field of stars, the entire expanse of the Milky Way and every star system humanity had ever visited or colonized. The other side was dark, inky blackness, a true void that her mind had trouble comprehending. Sure, if she looked in the right places she might see tiny smudges of color, all that the naked eye could see of other galaxies in their own corners of the universe. Except those were few and far between, doing little to relieve the disquiet from the reminder that she was quite literally on the edge of nothingness.

She could tell that the four hired mercenaries currently on the bridge, all official members of the crew unlike her, had similar feelings. The captain, Mart Lersson, sat in their chair absently picking at a piece of skin on their thumb. It was the quietest Vichna had seen Captain Lersson since meeting them thirteen standard days ago. On the other hand, the pilot, Elric Gregs, was uncharacteristically chatty, his voice providing a constant running commentary on everything from their speed to life sign readings. The latter, of course, was completely needless out here, but simply saying that there was nothing, or that nobody could live out here, seemed to help him deal with that fact.

Like Vichna, the two remaining people on the bridge didn't have to be here for this part. Also like her, they apparently hadn't been able to fight their curiosity. Both Bas Merton and Lussa Dakkenspear were here as security, the reason Vichna's backers had hired this particular mercenary team. They were the firepower in the unlikely event that they all came across something during the mission that required itchy trigger fingers. Vichna had protested using a team that included so many ex-marines and fleet members when she was helping put the mission together, but in the case of Lussa, at least, Vichna was glad her backers had outvoted her. In the previous two weeks, they had become close, even sharing a bed on occasion when the boredom of deep space got to them and they needed something (or someone) to do. Bas was a different story. Vichna couldn't exactly say she disliked him, but he came from a planet with some very old-fashioned views not shared by the rest of the mercenary crew. All attempts Vichna had made at talking to him had been tense, like at any moment he expected her to say something offensive so he could chew her out.

The only other person on the ship was Deck down in the engine room. He was an odd one, preferring to spend his time tinkering with the space-fold drive rather than hanging around anyone else, but during the few times Vichna had interacted with him, he'd been pleasant. Captain Lersson said he was the one on the ship with the experience in these deep space missions, and the sight of all the blackness had done strange things to his personality. Experiencing the emptiness herself now for the first time, Vichna could understand.

Captain Lersson looked her direction and must have seen something worrisome on her face. "It's not always this disturbing," they said. "You get used to it."

"How many times have you been out this far?" Vichna asked.

"This is my second time," Lersson said.

"But I thought you said Deck had been to the edge several times."

Gregs was the one who answered her. "Deck wasn't with the marines. He was with the fleet. He served on the *Merv Swansson* for three years."

Vichna certainly recognized the name of the ship. She should, considering the role it had played in the Violet and Lily Wars, which had been the subject of many of her studies. It annoyed her a little that they had such a notable veteran with them this whole time, yet no one had thought to tell her before now. Although part of that was her own fault, she supposed. The team knew that they'd been hired to escort her to find something, but to maintain secrecy, none of them had been told exactly what yet. Now they were here, though, practically on top of it from a galactic standpoint, and completely out of range for any kind of space-fold contact with any ship, colony, or inhabited planet.

"These are the correct coordinates I gave you?" Vichna asked the captain.

"We're coming up on them. Can you finally tell us what exactly we're looking for?"

"If you find something out here, anything at all, then obviously that's what we're here for."

"Then maybe we were paid to come out here for nothing, because I'm not seeing anything." There was a very clear note of frustration in the captain's voice, and Vichna couldn't blame them. All the people on the ship were right now on the very edge of the known galaxy. Here there were no outposts, no emergency supply caches, no help of any kind. It would have been dangerous if there were even anything out here to be afraid of, unless she counted the emptiness of space itself. If they went out any farther, they would vanish into the literal nothingness of the universe.

Which, of course, was why someone long ago had decided this would be the perfect hiding place.

"Finally picking up a faint radioactive signature," Gregs said from his console. "It's not much stronger than the background radiation. Probably wouldn't have noticed it if we weren't looking." He turned to Vichna. "Is that it?"

"I think so," she said. She actually knew so, but after so long searching for it, she almost felt afraid to jinx herself at the last moment.

"Visual?" Captain Lersson asked Gregs.

"It's still pretty far away," he said. "But whatever it is, it's big."

"How big?" Vichna asked.

"Similar to a decent-sized asteroid." He looked to her for confirmation that was correct, but Vichna couldn't speak. For most of her life, nearly one hundred and thirty-two years, she'd been looking for this. Granted, that only made her middle-aged, but sometimes it had felt like longer.

"So are you finally going to tell us what it is?" Lussa asked. "Or are you going to leave us guessing all the way up until the moment we can actually see it?"

"If I'm right, you'll want to wait," Vichna said. "This should be impressive. I hope."

"We've still got some distance to go yet before we'll even be able to make out details," Gregs said. "Want me to space fold until we're right next to it?"

The captain looked like they were about to okay this, but Vichna stopped them. "No! There... there might be some danger if we show up too suddenly." The captain shrugged. If anyone was upset at the idea that what they were here for might be dangerous, nobody showed it. They were usually paid for danger, after all, and they also had the mini-arsenal that her sponsors had paid to be brought along with them in the hold of the ship.

It took several more minutes before they were able to see anything with the naked eye, a problem caused by both the distance and the near-total lack of light. They had to rely on sensor images for most of the approach even as they got closer, and Vichna had the sensation of a large, invisible mouth approaching from ahead. Finally, they were close enough that the measly amount of light given off by their ship could be seen against the side of the approaching...

"Whoa," Merton said. "What even is that?"

"That" was a matte-black, blocky structure floating in the emptiness for no apparent reason. The design didn't look like anything special, or even functional for that matter. It looked like the designer (as the thing was definitely man-made) had simply taken a cube and then haphazardly continued to add smaller cubes to random places on its sides until the entire thing resembled a heavily-pixilated peanut. It would have seemed ridiculous if not for the enormous size of it. Gregs' estimation that it was the size of an asteroid wasn't far off, yet the thing still dwarfed their ship by a magnitude of about twenty or thirty. And even now, it was still hard to see, as whatever material it had been made out of was pure black and absorbed everything but direct light shined right upon it. Vichna looked to see if the structure had any thrusters or engines, something to indicate how it had been moved here in the first place, but there was nothing. She supposed it could have been built directly in this spot, although it was hard to imagine any construction team being able to stay sane in the emptiness long enough to finish it.

"This is really what we were hired to come out here and find?" the captain asked.

"Yes, this is it," Vichna said, not that she had ever seen it or even found a proper description of it. No one had, even if it was a fairy tale that everyone had heard at least once in their lifetimes. "It has to be. There's nothing else it *could* be."

"Well?" Merton asked. "Are you finally going to grace our ears with whatever secret you've been keeping?"

Vichna took a deep breath, less because she needed it and more for dramatic effect. "It's the Void."

Three of the four other people on the bridge reacted exactly the way she'd hoped they would. Captain Lersson turned to her with an expression that clearly said they didn't believe her. Gregs also stared at her but with his mouth agape. Merton just kept staring at the image on the screen in front of them. He was the only one on the ship with skin light enough for Vichna to see him visibly pale. Only Lussa looked confused.

"The Void?" she asked.

Vichna was about to answer but Merton beat her to it. "A space station. *The* space station. The one used by Captain Melissa Harvey."

"Oh," was all Lussa could say. That name she clearly recognized. Vichna would have been shocked if she hadn't. It did, after all, belong to the worst mass murderer ever known to the human race, a woman responsible for the complete genocide of eight entire star systems.

They all stared at the station floating outside their ship, a creation that most people only knew as something out of their nightmares. For many seconds, no one spoke.

Finally, Gregs said, "I thought it would be bigger."

2

Vichna was used to making presentations in front of an electric eye beaming her words out across forty-seven inhabited star systems. On rare occasions, she would even speak in a crowded lecture hall where thousands of people had paid good money to hear her drone on about the history of modern intergalactic warfare. It was a different thing entirely than what she was expected to do now: speak to five people sitting around a table in the small mess hall of the *Contra Besta* and explain to them finally why they were all here. Not that they didn't have a good guess by now.

"The Void?" Deck asked. His voice cracked as he spoke. Part of that was likely because of his obvious agitation, although some of it was also probably due to him starting GT, gender treatments, a few days earlier. Given a few more days, he would again be presenting himself as a woman instead of a man. Vichna felt bad about that. She would have liked to warn him earlier that their mission would likely be the kind where he didn't want the added stress of transitioning on top of everything else. That was why she herself had resisted the desperate need inside her to start her own treatments and spend some time as a man. Of course, she couldn't feel too sorry for him. Like most of the mercenary crew, he was ex-military, after all, so he should have known better. Modern military practices trained people to not switch at all unless they were absolutely sure they were out of stressful situations. The additional hormones produced during GT could sometimes cause complications no matter how efficient and safe the practice had become.

Deck stood up from his seat and gestured wildly in the air. "We seriously traveled to the ends of known space for the Void? Would you mind explaining to me why we haven't just blown it out of the sky yet?"

It was obviously a rhetorical question, since the *Contra Besta* was not currently capable of any such thing. While it was a model that could easily be fitted with any number of offensive and defensive weapons, that had been deemed by Vichna's investors to be an unnecessary expense. While there were a number of star systems that had adapted to a moneyless society, neither Vichna's partners nor any member of the crew were from them. Everyone here had been promised a payday, a big one, and she was sure they could all see by now that Vichna had not been kidding.

"We're not blowing anything up," Vichna said. "This is the most valuable archeological find of the last two hundred years."

"And were you actually around two hundred years ago, kid?" Deck asked. "I was little more than a child of forty when the Violet and Lily Wars broke out. I saw what that psychopath did. I actually had to help shovel the bodies at one point, because shoveling was the only way to carry something that was practically liquefied."

The captain gave Deck a stern look. "Deck, let's just hear what the professor has to say before we jump to any conclusions."

"Who's jumping to conclusions? I'm simply saying that it is not possible for anything good to come from Captain Harvey, so we shouldn't make any attempt to find it. Especially not in the Void, if that's what this place really is. You still haven't convinced me."

Vichna raised an eyebrow at the assertion that nothing good had ever come from the Pirate Queen of Deep Space, especially someone who was in the middle of his latest round of GT. Captain Melissa Harvey had been a brutal, disgusting human being, but she'd also been brilliant. Without her, there would have never been this technology that completely changed the entire course of human civilization.

The captain turned back to Vichna. "I'm assuming that, now that we're out of communication distance from anyone, you can finally tell us the whole story of why we're here?"

Vichna nodded. Usually, she had some kind of visual aid like hard-light holograms when she gave a lecture. Instead, she was going to have to make do for now without even her standard podium to hide behind. "Yes." She threw a pointed glare at Deck. "I'm assuming I'm not going to start by giving anyone here a basic history lesson about the Violet and Lily Wars, right?"

Deck glared right back at her, but didn't say anything. Everyone else at the table shook their heads. The main highlights were known to every person throughout the galaxy with even the most basic education. Before she'd given herself the title of pirate, Harvey had been a geneticist, which in itself had been thought of as a long-dormant discipline at the time. Harvey had changed that, showing there were still miracles to be discovered even long after the genomes of every known creature had been mapped. It was her who had discovered how to alter and reconfigure those most important foundations of human DNA, the X and Y chromosomes. The entire concept of gender had been thrown on its head. Now, people could change their physical sex at will, given a couple weeks to complete the process and some very mild discomfort. And that had been only the start of her research. Being able to change X and Y chromosomes led to other modifications being possible on a cellular level.

But when Melissa Harvey had reached her one seventy-ninth birthday, an age that had actually been considered old at the time, she'd snapped.

The Violet and Lily Wars were the result. That much was known by everyone, just as everyone knew that after thirty-six Sol standard years, the wars had finally ended when a coalition of twenty-eight star systems finally tracked down Captain Harvey's armada and obliterated every single ship, making sure that everything down to the leftover dust particles had been vaporized. The woman had been that dangerous.

Vichna, of course, knew a lot more than just those basics. "So tell me," she said, "what you all think you know as Harvey's time as the so-called Pirate Queen."

"I know that she had to have absorbed too many books to think that title made sense," Deck said.

"How do you mean?" Vichna asked. It was Gregs who responded.

"She had nothing to do with piracy. She was a crazed scientist who found a way to become a warlord, and then she butchered people. Her title was completely unrelated."

"That's what most people think, but there was more to it than that," Vichna said. "Now, I'll be the first to admit she was mad and there was nothing to emulate about her, but have you ever thought of her motivations?"

At first, it looked like no one was going to respond and Vichna would have to answer her own question until Merton spoke up.

"She thought she'd made a mistake. She was trying to undo what she had done with the first half of her life."

There was something in his tone that was vaguely unsettling, like he really did think there was something in Harvey's way of thinking that made sense. The others at the table looked just as uneasy, so Vichna decided to jump in before he could add anything more.

"It was a cleansing, she called it. When people could use her discoveries to change their genetics at will, to be able to alter hair color or skin color or gender whenever they wanted, she believed it had completely ceased evolutionary progress. Her exact words in her writings were that humanity had become a dead branch on the tree of life that needed to be pruned."

Instead of just interrupting, Lussa raised her hand, much to Vichna's amusement. "The thing I've never been able to understand is how she was able to get so many to join her. You would think that at least some of her followers would have realized that destroying all of humanity would include themselves."

Vichna pointed at her. "Right. That's a question a lot of people ask me, and I always say the same thing. They're making an incorrect assumption about the exact nature of her beliefs."

The captain chuckled humorlessly. "You mean there's something not to understand about wanting to obliterate every human in the Milky Way?"

"Except she didn't," Merton said. Again there was something dark about the way he said it that made Vichna's skin prickle, so she again spoke before he could continue.

"Harvey only wanted to kill anyone who had ever used her gene treatments. Those who abstained from using them were welcomed by her side and taught that they were the only ones who were on the evolutionarily correct track. You know, there have been some scholars over the years who have wondered why humanity didn't just abandon the concept of her gene treatments after Harvey went rogue, but I have a sociology professor friend that's writing a book saying that people used it as a general form of rebellion when…" She realized several sets of eyes at the table were glazing over. "You know what? Never mind. That has nothing to do with why we're here. But Lussa's question does."

This was the part where Vichna would have normally liked to have visual aids in her presentation, but she hadn't anticipated going into full-lecture mode while she was out here. "Captain Harvey wasn't just interested in preserving what she perceived to be pure, true humanity. She also wanted to preserve what she thought of as the pure *works* of humanity. Art, technology, architecture, films going all the way back to the time when they were made with actual film. Books, including physical, digital, and quantum versions. And most importantly to her, DNA samples. She had samples of every creature she could find throughout the galaxy, even down to bacteria and viruses."

"And human, I'm assuming?" Gregs asked. "Considering that was the one she seemed most obsessed with."

"Correct. DNA samples from all of her followers. What exactly she intended to do with them, no one has ever been able to say, since even cloning those she considered pure seems to have been against her beliefs. She kept all this pure material while using her technology to destroy all the rest. But, although it's well-documented that she collected all these things, it is hotly debated among historians where she actually kept it all."

"So wait, you're telling me that's what this is?" Lussa asked. "This Void place we've found is where she kept her plunder from around the galaxy?"

Vichna nodded. "That's why it is sort of correct to call her a pirate. She looted every world she destroyed, and all that loot had to go somewhere."

"But again, the Void is just a story, isn't it?" Gregs asked. "These things she took, it's most likely they were destroyed right along with her armada."

"And that's the prevailing theory among most historians. It's even what I believed for a time. Until I was given access to the original manuscript of *Pure Sterility*."

This time it was everyone else who gave *her* the nervous side-eyes she'd been giving Merton. On several of their home worlds, *Pure Sterility* was explicitly forbidden, and in several of the star systems that were still recovering from the Violet and Lily Wars two hundred years later, possession of Captain Melissa Harvey's treatise was an execution-worthy offense.

"Why would you even want to read that?" Lussa asked.

"I wasn't sure that I did. The original version of the manuscript is kept under lock and key at the Spatial Library on New Genysis. I was there researching other aspects of the war and hit a roadblock that I only thought I could get past if I saw the manuscript. It was so bizarre. The thing no one ever seems to realize is that it was written by hand. With ink. On paper, even."

"Ink?" Gregs asked. "What's that?"

"People long ago used to use it to make marks in order to communicate in written form," Vichna said. "It's a process that was obsolete long before Harvey was born. Even before humans left Earth. The language was at least modern, but beyond what can be found in the usual distributed version, there were also writings along the side of the paper, notes that she never included in the standard text and that she never intended anyone to see."

"And those notes told you to come here?" the captain asked.

Vichna shook her head. "No, but they implied that the Void was indeed a real place. There were notes on its construction, also some fragmented lists of what she intended to keep inside it, things she'd already taken at the time of the text's writing. Let's just say that what she had listed was… impressive. Impressive enough that I was able to bend a few wealthy ears and convince them to fund further research. It took decades of following leads, no matter how ridiculous they seemed. It was long enough that I myself began to doubt that what I was looking for even existed."

"It's kind of hard to believe that no one else ever found it, though," the captain said. "If there was a trail you could find, someone else could have as well."

"And yet if someone had found it before me, we would have heard about it. It's not the kind of thing most people would want to keep a secret. They'd want the fame and glory that came with finding so many priceless old artifacts. Even if someone had anonymously found it and sold what was inside, I've had contacts searching black markets for years looking for things that Harvey had on her list. None have ever shown up."

"So you really think we're the first people here in over two hundred years?" Lussa asked.

"Probably," Vichna said.

"If you're not expecting anyone to be here," Merton said, "then why would you hire a team of mostly former marines? And have us bring so much firepower?"

Vichna thought of the famed fierceness of Captain Harvey's acolytes. Every single last one of them had been a true believer. They had been willing to follow her without question even to the point where some stories, likely purely apocryphal, claimed that she would bring one or two of her followers along whenever negotiating. Then she would supposedly order them to slit their own throats as a show of their loyalty. It wasn't hard to imagine that she could have ordered some of her people to stay at the Void. Without standard gene treatments, those original people would be long dead. But her mind brought forth images of a lost tribe of people still living out here at the edge of the blackness, descendants of the original guards that still followed orders even to this day.

"We brought it," Vichna said, "just in case I'm wrong."

3

Their informal meeting had continued for another twenty minutes as they'd discussed the logistics of what exactly they were going to do here. They wouldn't actually make any attempt to enter the Void until Captain Lersson and Gregs had performed a thorough scan and sweep of the exterior, searching the entire thing for life forms or weapons systems. While they were doing that, the *Contra Besta* would keep a safe distance. Everyone else on the ship would have to hang tight for an hour or so until the captain declared it safe to board. Until then, Vichna had time to be alone with Lussa.

While every crew member had their own tiny room to themselves, Vichna had spent very little time on this mission in her own room unless she was working. She hadn't met any members of the crew before her backers had hired them, and for the most part, she hadn't made any effort to get to know them. Lussa, however, had been the only one to immediately recognize Vichna's name. By the end of the ship's first space fold, they'd struck up a rapport. By the end of the second, they were sleeping together.

The two of them lay naked in Lussa's bunk, each of them languidly caressing each other in post-orgasm bliss. Lussa made purring, contented noises against Vichna's shoulder, sounds that normally brought Vichna no end of happiness yet today troubled her. Now that they had actually found the Void, she had to start thinking about how things would be once they got back to civilization. For now, the crew seemed to be turning a blind eye to what was going on in this room during their free time, but Lussa had begun to talk as though their relationship would continue once this was over. But no one else would accept a middle-aged woman like Vichna having sex with a child-like Lussa. Hell, Lussa was only fifty-eight. Even the most backwards planet wouldn't consider Lussa an adult until she was sixty. If anyone outside the ship discovered what she had done with Lussa, then

Vichna's reputation would be ruined, at the least. At the worst, the minimum sentence for statutory rape was eighty years.

It was surprising that someone as young as Lussa was even part of the mission, let alone designated as security, and Vichna had commented on it during their conversations. Lussa had responded with pride that Vichna's backers had paid for the best. Vichna would have thought that undeserved boasting if the rest of the crew hadn't confirmed to her that yes, despite her ridiculously young age, Lussa was considered a prodigy with all forms of weapons as well as multiple forms of hand-to-hand combat. Vichna had no idea how anybody could be considered that good with only fifty-plus years of practice, but she had yet to find reason to question it even if she still hadn't seen Lussa in action.

Even though a part of her still insisted it was wrong, Vichna let her hand wander down to the warmth between Lussa's legs. The girl moaned and snuggled up closer against Vichna. Lussa had completed her latest GT just before the *Contra Besta* had launched, so her clitoris was still slightly elongated and bulbous after its recent time as a penis. Her labia had finally tightened back up from its previous existence as a scrotum, and her gonads were lodged back up inside her body, having long ago finished their transition from testes to ovaries. This was but one of the things that society accepted as normal that Melissa Harvey had rallied against. Lussa had originally been designated a girl at birth, but had told Vichna that she tended to spend most of her time as a male. She'd just decided on a whim before this mission that she had wanted to transition first. Vichna herself had changed genders so many times throughout her life that she didn't even remember what her original designation had been, nor did she usually take anyone seriously who thought such things mattered.

"Mmm, maybe you shouldn't do that," Lussa said, although the way she moved her hips against Vichna's hand suggested she might not be too serious. "Too much more and neither of us will have the energy to get up when the captain says it's okay to board the Void."

Simply saying the name of their target out loud made Vichna more focused. She took her hand away despite Lussa's incoherent protest.

"This is really it," Vichna muttered, more to herself than to Lussa. "After all this time, I'm finally going to see what's inside."

Realizing that their love-play was really over, Lussa pulled away from Vichna to stretch, cracking her well-defined back muscles.

"You really don't think there's going to be anything to worry about in there, do you?" she asked. Lussa's tone suggested she herself didn't see any reason to worry. Vichna generally agreed. Her dark fantasy about a lost band of Harvey's elite was likely nothing more than a product of her over-active imagination. Nothing in the literature or legends Vichna had found suggested anything of the sort. Then again, what little she *had* found had been maddeningly incomplete. Vichna couldn't imagine someone like Harvey leaving the Void completely unprotected, although the vast expanse of emptiness just outside the ship's hull was probably protection enough. It had concealed this place for over two hundred years, after all.

"No, we'll probably be fine, although getting through whatever locks Captain Harvey had in this thing will likely be tricky."

"Why didn't you tell me from the beginning that this was what we were looking for?"

Lussa stood up and turned to Vichna. Her naked body was truly something to behold, and it had little to do with whatever gene work she'd had done. The chocolate-brown of her skin was common on her home planet, Lussa said, and not altered like Vichna's own color. Her muscles were the product of much hard work and training rather than a few pills. She was gorgeous, stunning, incredibly attractive. Yet the pouty way she stood left no doubt that she had a lot of maturing to do. Long ago, some time even before Melissa Harvey and her amazing technologies, Lussa might have been considered old at this point. But when it was possible for a modern person to live as long as three and fifty years, society adjusted its beliefs about age accordingly.

"Are you upset about that?" Vichna asked.

"Well, yes. Of course. I thought you trusted me. It wasn't like I would have told."

"It's not that I didn't trust you. It's just..." Well, it was that Vichna didn't trust her, but that wasn't any fault of Lussa's. This had been her project for so long that she'd become paranoid that someone else would follow the same trail of breadcrumbs and claim all the glory for themselves. It was the culmination of her life's work, but there were trillions of people throughout the galaxy who could have found it before her. The possibility had kept her awake many nights. Even after she'd secured the financial backing and gotten under way on the *Contra Besta*, she'd still worried that something would go wrong and everything she'd done with her life would be worth nothing.

"I suppose I don't really blame you for keeping quiet, though," Lussa said. "Especially considering Bas." She bent to the floor to pick up her clothes as Vichna sat up in bed.

"Bas? What about him?" Vichna asked. She supposed it was not coming back to bite her in the ass that she hadn't bothered to spend much time with the rest of the crew. First there was all she could have learned from Deck, now apparently this.

"You know he's Cetian, right?"

Vichna nodded. That much had been obvious to her before anyone had said anything else about him. The majority of the original settlers of Tau Ceti had been pale-skinned and also extremely religious. The religious beliefs, although they had changed over time, had nonetheless informed their culture to make many of the cities on the planet some of the most conservative in the galaxy. This conservatism, in turn, had made them slow to embrace the societal change that swept through all the inhabited planets following Melissa Harvey's discoveries. It had become a stereotype, sometimes true and sometimes not, that the notable fair skin of a Cetian meant a person would be humorless and disapproving of gender transitioning. As such, Vichna had simply assumed that Bas Merton not only had been male for a long time, but might even have never actually undergone GT in his entire life.

It was also believed (although as a historian Vichna knew it was more complicated than that) that an abnormally large number of Captain Harvey's forces had been recruited from Tau Ceti. Vichna immediately thought she knew where Lussa was going with this.

"It's not exactly fair to distrust him because of that, though,"

Vichna said. "Besides, my backers did a very thorough background check on every person on this team. They cleared him. And trust me, there was a very long list of mercenary teams and former marines that didn't make the cut."

"How old do you think he is?" Lussa asked.

Vichna had no idea what that had to do with anything, but she didn't see the harm in taking an educated guess. "Um, he looks a little older than me, so I'm going to say a hundred and fifty."

"He's actually seventy-six. You just thought he's twice as old as he actually is."

That startled Vichna. "How can that be possible?" Even as she asked, she thought she already knew the answer. Predominant Cetian beliefs may have been that gender treatments were decadent or immoral, yet few of them seemed to have problems with any gene treatment that slowed aging or prolonged life. There were, however, a few radical sects that occasionally made the news feeds.

"His family apparently brought him up with the Purser Sect. I don't know if you've ever heard of them. I sure hadn't. But they believe that any manipulation of genes at all is an affront to their guardian spirits or something. The only reason he doesn't already look like a scraggly old man is because they still allow for a very few non-genetic treatments."

Suddenly, Vichna understood why Lussa was so concerned about him being involved. Those beliefs seemed suspiciously close to those of Harvey's followers.

"But you've been a part of this team for a while now, haven't you?" Vichna asked. "Aren't most ex-military types big on trusting the people next to them?"

"You know, I skipped the part about being a marine or in the fleet. I'm still the young blood to them, and I don't have the same side-by-side experience that some of them do."

"I understand your worry, but I have the utmost trust in the people I had vetting him. And even if they somehow missed something relevant to his background, I still don't think there's any particular problem that could arise with him. We're talking about a space station potentially full of archeological items and museum pieces."

"I suppose," Lussa said, her voice both sullen and unconvinced.

"Hey, don't finish putting your clothes on yet," Vichna said. "Come here." She gestured for Lussa to once more join her on the bed. After a few seconds of hesitation, Lussa crawled back onto the sheets.

"Nothing's going to go awry," Vichna said. "Everything about this entire expedition has been planned by my people down to the letter." She realized that it was odd that she was comforting one of her security people regarding their degree of safety, yet it felt natural to get Lussa back into her arms and squeeze her tight.

"Yeah, I suppose," Lussa said again, this time with more feeling. At the same time, her hand slipped down to Vichna's belly button and started playing with it. Vichna cooed contentedly and encouraged her to continue. Let the worries about their relationship wait until later. Now was just the time to enjoy it.

4

"I think it's somehow managed to get blacker," Deck whispered.

Vichna filled the air with words about how that was ridiculous, how the Void was still the exact same color it had been a couple of hours ago when they had found it. She even believed them. Yet she had to admit that it *felt* darker, like it had been absorbing any and all light they shone at it in order to transmogrify it into something darker even than black. It almost hurt the eyes and mind to look at it. Did it have some kind of special property that caused this effect? Had Captain Harvey imbued it with some previously unknown technology? Or was this all just a trick of their brains, a reaction to the absolutely lightless background farther beyond the Void? Neither possibility was particularly comforting.

They were all once again on the bridge of the *Contra Besta*, even Deck, who really should have been down in the engine room. The captain and Gregs had completed their scans and declared the Void to be absent of both external weapons and life. They were picking up odd energy readings throughout the entire station, however. Vichna took that to mean the Void had a working power source and its internal functions might still be running after two hundred years, but they couldn't find the exact source of the power. That in itself was odd, considering the *Contra Besta*'s sensors were state of the art and should have easily been able to scan technology that was a couple centuries out of date. And yet something in the Void's outer hull diffused their scanning beams, giving them only a hazy idea at best of which areas were receiving power and which were dormant.

"If the Void is somehow preventing us from finding its exact power source, then how sure can we be that the other scans were correct?" Merton asked.

"They run on different principles to detect different things," Lersson said with a wave of their hand. "You don't need to worry."

Vichna had to wonder, but Lersson seemed confident. If the captain trusted those readings, then Vichna figured she should as well.

"Did you find any entrances?" Vichna asked. "Or maybe any sort of specialized outside structures at all? Something that could tell us anything about how the Void got here and what it's capable of?"

"There are trace amounts of debris in the surrounding area. Very small, with trace radiation that suggests it was part of something that was vaporized."

"By a Higgs beam, perhaps?" Vichna asked the question cautiously. Higgs beams were outlawed in all star systems, mostly because of the monumental amount of damage they had done during the Violet and Lily Wars. Harvey had been known to use them once or twice but overall had dismissed them as inelegant. It was a prejudice that got the better of her eventually, considering Higgs beams had been one of several weapons that had led to her armada finally being wiped out.

"No, a Higgs beam would have made it impossible for us to even determine the elements present in the debris. The little bit we've found seems consistent with a destroyed ship or possibly what equipment was used to build the Void in the first place."

So it was probably built right here, Vichna thought. Harvey destroyed most of the evidence of it, and most likely anyone unlucky enough to have been involved in the construction.

"Anything else?" Vichna asked.

"Nothing we can see that suggests a mode of movement," Gregs said. "This thing isn't going anywhere without the help of several enormous tow ships. No noticeable communication equipment, or at least not on the outside. Either there's something on the inside that we've never seen before or there's no way to send and receive messages, but that's not surprising given how far out we are." He paused to take a closer look at the readings shown on his display. "Density of the entire thing appears to be inconsistent. It's difficult to tell, since the station must have some kind of shielding, but it looks like this place has a number of smaller rooms and then several much larger rooms. No indication of what's in any of them."

Again Vichna felt a little bit of concern regarding the lack of clarity in some of the readings. One wrong reading could always mean that others were wrong, too, and they wouldn't be any wiser. "All right. Then what about entrances?"

"We've detected a number of small anomalies at seemingly random points along the outside." He touched a few points in his display, and a three-dimensional hard-light representation of the Void appeared just over their head. The outer hull showed up as blue while a number of red dots pocked the surface. Gregs was right. There didn't seem to be any rhyme or reason to their placement. "Judging roughly by their shape, I'd guess they're either escape pods or emergency hatches, although I don't know what good any of those would do somebody. If a person had to get out of there in a hurry, they would still be out of luck if they didn't have a vehicle with a space fold engine. All they'd end up doing is floating away into nothing."

Vichna felt a shiver at that thought. She looked around and saw that she wasn't the only one.

"More importantly, though, is this," Gregs said as he touched the display again. A large, bright patch appeared on the Void's underside (or at least it appeared to be the underside from this angle, since in the disorientation of space it could have been the front, back, or even top for all they knew). Vichna moved closer to the projection and studied the highlighted area.

"Looks to me like it could be some kind of door," she said.

"That's what we thought, too," the captain said. "If you look at it, it seems to open down the center. We weren't able to exactly identify what that structure is around it, but our best guess is that it serves as an air seal against docking ships."

Vichna nodded. "That would be consistent with the state of technology that Harvey was working with at the time."

Lussa finally spoke. "So that's the front door."

"As best as we can tell," the captain said.

"Please for the love of all that's holy tell me that we're not planning on going in through there," Deck said.

Vichna turned to him. "How else would you propose we get in?"

"I don't propose we get in at all! Didn't I make that clear enough already? Nothing good can possibly come from there. But if you really, really want to go in then don't be idiots. The absolute last thing you want to do walk through the spot that practically has 'Come in here' written on it in hard-light."

"I'm still not hearing a proposal for a different path," Vichna said, her voice reflecting her growing impatience.

"I don't know. Blow a hole open in the side. Build a matter transmitter from a soup can and teleport yourself. I don't care. Just don't go waltzing right through the front door. Why is it even necessary to go in right now, anyway? You've found it. Congratulations! Now's the time to go back to someplace inhabited, get your financial backers to give you an army, and then come back when you have massive firepower trained on the place in the case that it so much as bobs in space the wrong way."

"We can't just go back without exploring further," Lussa said. She looked to Vichna. "Can we?"

Vichna was about to say simply that this wasn't a democracy, that she was paying them and they would do whatever she asked. But she had to admit there was a small amount of sense to what he said. She'd led them out here because she was certain there was something to find, but the Void was beyond all expectations. There was no telling what might be inside beyond a simple treasure trove. There was a very real possibility of danger. But then again, that was why they had come prepared and armed. Vichna also couldn't get over the paranoid possibility that, if they went back now, news of what they had found would leak before they could return. She could think of nothing worse than returning and finding it swarming with the ships of opportunistic treasure hunters, plundering the Void with no respect for its historical value.

Besides, Lussa was right. Her curiosity wouldn't allow her to come this far and then turn around. She wouldn't be satisfied until she knew what was inside.

"We already have everything we need to deal with any potential problems," Vichna said. "We'll be fine. But that's only if we can actually get in. We may have found the front door, but I highly doubt Harvey just left it unlocked. Have you figured out what kind of security we're looking at on that thing yet?"

"We were waiting for your go-ahead before we tried anything," the captain said. They paused as though debating something in their head before speaking again. "I would just like to state for the record that I share some of Deck's hesitancy. You may be our employer, but I'm still captain of this ship and mission. And if at any point I decide the risk is too great, I'm calling the entire thing off. Do you understand? You may have your own priorities, but mine are to the safety of this crew."

"I understand," Vichna said. And she wasn't just saying that. She was fully aware that her emotions were running the show right now. As much as she wanted to believe she was a person purely of reason and logic, emotions were simply not something humans had evolved beyond, like they had the need for static gender or race. If the captain decided she wasn't thinking clearly about the subject, then their word would be law.

"Okay then," the captain said. Despite their words, Vichna could tell that Lersson was just as excited about this as she was. "Let's see what we can do about walking up to the front door and knocking."

5

The *Contra Besta* approached the "front door" slowly, wary of the possibility that there was some sort of security or weapon system that they had missed. Vichna certainly had to admit that this was the entrance the Void's designer had wanted people to use, which only made them more leery. While the rest of the station was matte black, the door was a dull gray. In any other environment, the color would have been uninviting, but against the rest of the Void and the emptiness beyond, it was practically a beacon lighting up the sky. Scans didn't show any way of manually opening it from the outside, though.

"Did your research give you any clues about what to do next?" the captain asked.

Vichna had to think about that one. None of the few scraps of information she'd found about the Void said anything about how to get in. But she had also studied Harvey enough that she believed any relevant information had to be in her mind somewhere. She just had to figure out what it was.

"Is there any way we can send some kind of signal to it?" Vichna asked.

The captain shook their head. "We scanned for all that before. There was nothing."

"Were you only scanning for the sorts of signals or devices we use now? Or were you taking into account what Harvey might have used instead two hundred years ago?"

The captain blinked. "I can't believe I didn't think of that. Gregs, search for…" They paused, looking at Vichna for some idea of what specifically to search for. Deck answered first. Although he wasn't on the bridge anymore, he was evidently still listening to their conversation from the engine room.

"Try a trace-epsilon signature," Deck said through the comm. "That's where we eventually found her signals near the tail end of the wars."

Gregs scanned and, sure enough, they began hearing a series of rapid-fire clicks over the com systems.

"What the hell is that?" Merton asked. "Sounds like someone's slaughtering a fishnic."

"It's a code," Vichna said. "Captain, do you have anything on old Violet and Lily codes in the ship's databanks?"

"We should," Captain Lersson said. "Gregs, run it through a translator."

He did, and the clicks turned into a repeating monotone message in a female voice. "Perfect sequence. Perfect sequence. Perfect sequence."

"Oh dear spirits protect us," Deck whispered through the com. "It's like hearing a ghost."

"What? What's wrong?" Lussa asked.

"That's Melissa Harvey's voice," Vichna said. Several of the people on the bridge noticeably tensed. Merton, she noticed, was not one of them. "It's just a recording." That much should have been obvious, although Vichna realized she was saying it more for her own benefit than for anyone else. Vichna had heard plenty of recordings of Harvey's voice during her years of study. In fact, she felt confident in saying that she had heard every known recording of the woman ever made. Simply hearing her voice again, now, using words and tone that no one had heard in two hundred years, was disconcerting even for her. The tone in this recording, though, was highly peculiar. The monotone clearly suggested an artificial message not directly recorded by Harvey herself, as though it were some computer's approximation of her voice. Except that didn't make a lot of sense, since even in Harvey's time an AI would have been more advanced than that.

Captain Lersson must have been thinking along the same lines. "Did Harvey have the same problem with AIs that she did with the genetically altered?"

Vichna shrugged. "Her relationship with the AI Collective was very complicated."

Gregs turned to look at her. "Wait, she was in contact with the AI Collective itself?"

"Supposedly. But if there's any exact records of those meetings either they were never found or the Collective has them all." Lussa gave her a questioning look, and Vichna told her she'd explain more later. Lussa wasn't exactly a student of history or politics, so Vichna couldn't be sure how much she knew about the AI Collective, but truthfully even someone like Vichna couldn't be said to know that much. The AI Collective kept to themselves and rarely took any interest at all in the affairs of humans. The history of the Collective had begun long before Melissa Harvey and her gene treatments. They even had their origins before Earth was left behind in the mass colonizations. When true AI had been developed, humans had been their typical paranoid selves and tried to regulate it, something that obviously didn't go over well with the newborn artificial life forms. But rather than fulfilling the long-held prophecy that robots would turn on their human masters, they had surprised everyone by leaving humanity completely. Every attempt to develop new AI after that met with mysterious sabotage or else the AI vanishing soon after. Humans had eventually stopped messing with artificial intelligence altogether, or at least any AI that could be truly considered sentient. The exact location of all these AIs somewhere out in the galaxy was a mystery to all but a few notable heads of state, or so they claimed. The entire existence of the AI Collective might be considered a myth if not for the fact that, every few hundred years, they got in contact with a person they found interesting.

"So are we listening to an actual AI then, or something else?" the captain asked as the voice continued repeating its phrases.

"I highly doubt it's a full AI," Vichna said. "Something more primitive like..." She tried to think back much further in the depths of time than normal, looking for the name of a technology that was comparable. Siri, she remembered. Or maybe Cortana. But she didn't think either of those names would have any meaning to the rest of the crew. "...like something that's designed to sound like a personal assistant even though it's really just feeding back canned responses."

"So Harvey made her fake personal assistant sound exactly like her?" Gregs asked. "Now there's an ego."

"Why does it keep saying that, though?" the captain asked. "What does 'perfect sequence' mean?"

Vichna thought about it for a moment. The word "sequence" only brought one thing to mind when she thought of Captain

Melissa Harvey. Could the answer really be that easy? Well, actually she supposed it wasn't supposed to be easy at all.

"It's asking for a password," Vichna said. "And I think I know it. Or at least I think I have it." She quickly ran back to her quarters and found all the thumbscans containing the terabytes of data she had on Harvey and the Violet and Lily Wars. There was one piece of data in here that she'd never found the need to thoroughly go over. She would need it now.

After isolating what she needed on a single thumbscan, she went back to the bridge and had Gregs feed the scan into the computer.

"What is this?" he asked hesitantly before uploading it.

"'Perfect sequence' refers to a gene sequence. Specifically, I think, hers. Her complete genetic sequence is the password to get into the Void."

"Why would you even have that?" the captain asked.

"I used it as an example during New Genisys's last public hearing on whether to re-legalize cloning. My argument was that her sequence is known public data that can be found if someone knows where to look. It would be very easy for some zealot to try to bring her back as a clone."

"That wouldn't really be her, though," the captain said. "It would be someone with the same genes, but not the same experiences."

Deck spoke again through the comm. "Do you really think that would matter to some rabid fringe organization? They would just need the clone as a figurehead to rally her followers behind. And trust me, there are still followers."

Vichna looked at Merton as Deck said this, but Merton didn't react. If anything, he looked a little bored.

"So she thought her own gene sequence was the perfect one?" Lussa asked. "Gregs was right. That really was a huge ego."

"Before I send this as a signal to the station, are you sure this is going to be safe?" Gregs asked.

Vichna looked at the captain without saying anything. Lersson stared back for a moment before nodding. Of course she couldn't be sure this was safe. Nothing about this could really be called safe. And that made it the captain's final call whether or not they went forward.

"Go ahead, Gregs," the captain said. "In the meantime, I want everyone else suited up to board that thing. And I want everyone armed."

Vichna started to object. "I don't think I'm really going to need..."

"My ship, my rules, professor. We already went over that. And in this case, my rule is that anyone who goes anywhere near that thing is armed. Understood?"

Given how close she was to finally getting inside, Vichna decided this was not the time to argue. "Understood, Captain."

"Okay then," Gregs said. "Translating the sequence back into the codes and trace-epsilon signature. And... sending."

Despite the captain's order that they all start prepping, no one moved as they listened to the A's, C's, G's, and T's of Melissa Harvey's genetic code became an incredibly long series of incomprehensible clicks.

"The signal from the Void is stopping," Gregs said. "Wait, no. It's changing."

The harsh, smoky monotone that was the fake Captain Harvey echoed throughout the ship. "Sequence accepted. Welcome back to the Void, Melissa."

6

It wasn't too much for Vichna to adjust to the survival suit hugging her skin. She'd had to wear one on many occasions in the past, usually when surveying the lost wreckage of a Violet and Lily era warship found floating through space. The suit looked like nothing more than an incredibly thin layer of flimsy, almost see-through material stretched over her body, but even if its looks did little to inspire confidence, Vichna knew from experience that the suit adjusted almost instantly to any extreme. She could get flash frozen yet still feel warm and toasty, then immediately afterward fall into an active volcano and still survive for several minutes before the lava managed to eat through the material. Of course, none of these things would work if she wasn't wearing the helmet properly, but Captain Lersson themself went to each person and double-checked the seals on the helmets.

What Vichna had more trouble acclimating to was the enormous rifle in her hands. She knew how to use it in theory, and Lussa assured her that this model was about as new-user friendly as they could get, but its weight still felt awkward. And she didn't even have the biggest gun. That honor belonged to Lussa and Merton, both of whom carried weapons large enough that they needed to be mounted to thin exoskeletons that bonded to the outside of their survival suits.

"Don't we at least have something smaller?" Vichna asked. "Something like a pistol? I do have to carry my other equipment as well." She indicated the small satchel on the floor next to her. It contained a data unit with as much of her research on Harvey and the Void as it could carry, a small scanner and DNA tester, and a number of emergency survival supplies that she had found helpful in the past.

"If something goes wrong, you would probably prefer the rifle," Lussa said, but she nonetheless pulled a laser pistol from the weapons locker and handed it to Vichna along with a holster. Vichna put the rifle back and then strapped the holster around her hip. She was the only one opting for a smaller weapon, she saw. Both Captain Lersson and Deck selected rifles. Vichna wasn't sure if it was a good idea for all of them to board the Void at once, but the captain had insisted on being with their crew and it had been decided that Deck might be needed if they ran into any problems that were mechanical in nature. Gregs would be the only one remaining on the *Contra Besta* for the time being, ensuring the ship remained prepped and ready should they need to leave in a hurry. Vichna was still torn on whether or not this was a necessary precaution, but it had been the captain's orders, so she didn't have any say in it.

Once they were all suited up and had their equipment in order, they made their way to the emergency cargo hatch. It was the only exit that was the proper size to fit the seal of the Void's front door. Gregs had moved them within docking range while they changed, and now that they were at the door, they could feel the slight thump throughout the ship as the seal locked between the two vessels.

"Helmets on, everyone," Lersson said. "It's not likely the air in there is going to be breathable after two hundred years."

Vichna wasn't so sure about that, given the abnormally high level of technology Harvey always seemed to have at her disposal. That didn't mean they shouldn't be cautious, though.

"Seal's tight," Gregs said over the comm. "You're all go to enter the airlock."

The massive inner cargo door opened and they all stepped through. Once the door shut, there was a hiss as the air from the *Contra Besta* cycled out and the Void's air cycled in. The fact that they could hear air coming in at all meant there at least was some in the Void and it hadn't experienced some sort of decompression over the many years.

Lights flashed inside the captain's helmet as they brought up a readout. "Looks like the air would be breathable in an emergency."

Vichna brought up her own readout to flash across her eyes from the helmet's visor. Lersson was right that they could breathe the air, although it was thin and would likely make them light-headed. It was better to leave their helmets on for now. She also searched for any sign of airborne pathogens, but as far as her suit could tell, there was nothing.

"Looks like we're okay to open the outer door," the captain said. Gregs gave an affirmative and a yellow light flashed in the airlock as the door slowly ground open, the door to the Void opening right along with it. Vichna held her breath in the strobing light, anxious for her first glimpse into what might as well have been the largest time capsule ever created.

Although outside noises were muted somewhat by her helmet, Vichna could hear the way sounds echoed just beyond as the door opened into a darkness almost as total as that outside. Only the echo kept her from thinking something had gone wrong and they were about to be vented into the emptiness outside the galaxy. There might not have been light, but there was definitely a room beyond, and an enormous one at that.

"I'm reading a gravity equal to standard in there," the captain said. "Whatever life support is in this place, at least the gravity generators still work. Although... these readings are strange."

"How so?" Lussa asked. Rather than wait for the answer, Vichna brought the gravity up on her own display. There appeared to be multiple small-level anomalies some distance away. Although the captain said this out loud to Lussa, none of them could figure out what that meant.

The door finished cycling open, yet none of them moved. All the others kept their weapons ready, but Vichna didn't bother to draw hers. She doubted there would be any sort of threat right at the front gate that could be taken care of with rifles and pistols. All thoughts of a lost group of acolytes waiting to pounce on them had vanished. There was no one here. It hadn't been home to life for a long time. Now was the moment for all of them to get over their paranoia, instead embracing that they were making history right now: the first people to find the lost treasure of the Pirate Queen.

"I'm not picking up anything on your cameras yet," Gregs said. "What are you all seeing?"

Vichna was the first to advance through the door into the cavernous room beyond. Or at least she assumed it was cavernous, since it was still pitch black. After adjusting some controls on her helmet, everything brightened slightly, her visor now in low-light mode, but even that didn't help much when there was no light at all. Finally, she had to use the most primitive of her tools, the actual light protruding from the top of her helmet.

"It doesn't look like there's a lot to see just yet," the captain said. "There's walls some distance away. They look like they might be either gray or blue. I don't see any structures or furnishings in here."

"No movement on any of the sensors," Lussa said. "The only heat signatures I seem to be picking up look like they're coming from the walls. Must be whatever's powering the life support."

"Well, Professor? You're up," Merton said. "This is your show and you're the expert. What do we do from here?"

That was a good question, and Vichna had to admit that she was so overwhelmed that she didn't have an answer. To be the first people here in over two hundred years was astounding. And the size of this place! Obviously, she had known intellectually that it was big just by seeing it from the outside, but it felt like entirely different knowledge from where she was standing. Had the Void really only been used to store Captain Harvey's ill-gotten gains? If so, then there had to be more here than she had been led to believe by Harvey's notes. The other option was that this place had also been used for something else, but Vichna still couldn't imagine what.

"My first guess for any place from this time would be that there's an information terminal or kiosk somewhere," Vichna said. "That's how other space stations were designed."

"Yeah? Well, this hardly like other stations, is it?" Deck asked. Vichna nodded in silent agreement.

She took a look at the energy and heat signatures. Anything being built today would have enough shielding that she wouldn't see the blurs in the walls denoting power lines or sources, but here they showed up as dull blue smears against the otherwise dark walls and floor panels. There were many of them leading up to the door they had just come through and many that tapered away into the floor, presumably powering the artificial gravity. She noticed one line slightly brighter than the others, though, and as she followed it along the floor, she thought she could see the energy signatures pulsing.

"What is it?" Lussa asked as she followed behind. Vichna looked back to see everyone else had formed a line behind her, and with the exception of Merton, who continually searched the area around them for threats, they all stared down at the same power line as her.

"It's powering something other than basic functions, I think," Vichna said. The line stopped at what Vichna guessed was more or less the center of the room. In fact, several lines converged here. Vichna knelt down to take a closer look at the slightly-raised circular platform all the lines led into.

"Looks like a hard-light generator," Lersson said. "Old model. Haven't seen anything like that since I was a child."

Vichna agreed. Based on her own memories, as well as her knowledge of Harvey's time, this couldn't be anything better than a second-generation, hard-light generator. That was when they had started to figure out how to make hard-light actually "hard," at least figuratively speaking. While current fifth-level generators, when given enough power, could create actual physical tactile objects in addition to holograms, second-level generators had been the first where, if one touched the image it created, one could feel a small amount of sensory feedback. Touch an image of a sand castle and one could swear that it felt gritty, even as the person's fingers pushed right through the image.

"I don't see anything else in the entire room," Merton said. "Doesn't that seem odd to anyone? An enormous room purely for one hard-light generator?"

"Yes, I'd agree it's odd," Vichna said. "But I would also venture a guess that it's far from the oddest thing we'll see in this station."

"See if you can turn it on," the captain said.

Deck responded with a distinct choking noise. "Or we could maybe not go pushing random buttons in the top secret hideout of the galaxy's most notorious mass murderer." Deck turned his rifle in the direction of the generator. He kept his finger off the trigger, but he was obviously ready to melt the generator into slag if it so much as burped at him. Vichna gently pushed the barrel away.

"It will be easier for us to get around if we can restore power to some of the other systems, like lights. Since this is the only non-essential thing that looks active, we have to start here."

Deck pointed his rifle away from the generator, although he still kept a death grip on the barrel.

Vichna leaned down to examine the generator closer. It didn't appear damaged in any way, so it should work if she could turn it on, but there was no switch or power button anywhere around it. There were a couple of small devices that might have been sensors, however. She waved her hand over them, but they did nothing. Not motion activated, then. Perhaps it was voice activated?

"Hello?" she asked the sensor. Nothing happened. "Can you hear me? Computer? Assistant?"

"If the voice we heard earlier was some kind of virtual assistant," Lersson said, "then maybe it doesn't activate until you say its name."

Although that sounded likely to Vichna, she didn't have the slightest clue where to begin guessing. She reached back into her memories for virtual assistants from the deep past. "Siri? Cortana? Morgenstern? Lufi?"

The generator remained inactive.

"Maybe she named it after someone that was important to her," Lussa said. "Did she have anyone like that?"

"Sort of," Vichna said. "She had a small number of trusted lieutenants." Vichna listed out loud all the names she could think of. Still no response.

"This is getting us nowhere," Merton muttered.

"Just wait," Vichna said. "I'm sure we're on the right track." She had to access her thumbscan for more names. She tried Harvey's parents, the man she'd supposedly been romantically linked to when she'd died, her first known boyfriend, even the virtual cockatiel she'd had as a pet when she was a kid.

"Maybe this is a dead end," Lersson said. "It's not like Harvey was even the kind of person to have anyone important to her."

"Everyone has someone they think is important," Vichna said. "Even if it's just..." Wait. Could it really be that simple and easy? She thought back to the voice they'd heard before entering and wanted to hit herself for not thinking of it sooner.

Vichna stood up and addressed the generator. "Melissa." The generator didn't turn on, but this time at least it emitted a feeble electronic *blat* noise. She assumed that was its way of telling her that was the wrong answer. At least she was on the right track.

"Harvey?"

Blat.

"Melissa Harvey."

Blat.

"Captain Melissa Harvey."

Blat.

Vichna sighed. There was only one more possible answer. Again with the woman's ego.

"Captain Melissa Harvey, Pirate Queen of Deep Space."

The generator whirred and came to life.

Captain Harvey stood before them.

Everyone's guns but Vichna's immediately went up. Deck cursed and looked like he was the closest to pulling the trigger when Vichna jumped in front of him.

"Wait! For great mana's sake, wait, all of you. It's obviously not really her. Just take a step back and breathe, okay?"

Everyone lowered their weapons, Deck of course being the last. Hard-light hologram or not, he was obviously not comfortable being in the same room with any representation of this woman. Vichna, however, turned back to the hologram with absolute wonder.

The quality of the hologram was striking for only a second-generation generator. It was missing most of the fuzzy blue glow typical of hard-light images of the time, instead having a near-perfect clarity that was rare even today. The only giveaway that this wasn't a live person standing in front of them was the image's slight translucence. Vichna circled it, finding she could just barely see the others through it on the other side.

But the image's quality wasn't even the most amazing part. This was her, Captain Melissa Harvey, exactly as she had been when she was alive. Vichna knew most of the woman's physical details from various recordings she'd watched over the years, but this image caught things all the others missed. Harvey wore a white, long-sleeved shirt and a tight black leather vest – real leather, the kind that had been illegal even in Harvey's day – that accentuated her slim figure and small breasts. Her leggings and boots were also black, but made in an archaic lace-up fashion. Probably to create more of the pirate feel, Vichna figured. Her dark blonde hair was pulled back into a tight, utilitarian braid. Her skin, pale and pink, had an intense flushed look that made her permanently look like she had just gone for a run. Or had sex. Vichna herself felt her cheeks grow warm and hoped no one else could notice. The last thing she needed was the team to think she found the worst person in the history of mankind to be attractive.

For a moment, they all waited for the hologram to say something. When it became apparent that it wouldn't do anything without further input, Vichna put out her hand to touch it. There was a crackling noise and her hand moved through it, but with the gloves on her survival suit, she couldn't feel anything. Vichna peeled the glove off her left hand.

"Wait, don't do that," Lersson said.

"I'll put it back on right away. I promise. I just want to be sure it's a generation two." In truth what she wanted to know was what this woman she'd spent most of her life studying had actually felt like. She admitted it was a strange desire, but sometimes it was easy to forget that all the history with which she surrounded herself had actually happened, that it was more than just an intellectual exercise. That Harvey, every person she'd killed, and every person who had died in the Violet and Lily Wars, had been a true flesh and blood person.

Not that this hologram was flesh and blood either, but it was the closest Vichna would ever get to Melissa Harvey.

She put her finger to the hologram's cheek. As it passed through the light, she had the briefest sensation of soft flesh, then a slightly unpleasant tingle. She pulled her hand back and put the glove back on, although the tingle remained for nearly a minute.

"Okay, so we've made this… thing appear," Deck said. "Now what?"

"Now we ask her questions," Vichna said. "Melissa?"

The hologram turned to her with an expression of innocent curiosity that Vichna had a hard time imagining on the real Captain Harvey's face.

"How may I help you?"

"What can you tell us about this place?"

"Please be more specific."

"Is this or is this not the Void?"

The hologram cocked her head. "Yep."

"That's a strangely informal answer for a virtual assistant, I would think," Lersson said.

The hologram turned to them. "I'm programmed to respond the way the captain would in almost every situation."

"Now there's a truly scary thought," Deck said.

"Relax," Vichna said. "Remember, she's just an assistant. She's not even a true AI. She's limited to small number of canned, preprogrammed responses."

The hologram turned to her again and flashed a smile that was disturbingly close to the real thing. Vichna had seen it in several recordings just before Harvey had slaughtered entire cities. "That's an awful lot of assumptions you're making. You know what they say about assuming. It makes an ass out of you and then something horribly painful happens."

Gregs' voice came in over their comms. "Um, everyone? I might not have understood what that meant, but it didn't sound like a canned response to me."

Vichna got a sinking, hard feeling in her gut. He was right. If that was programmed, then her possible responses were more extensive than she would have expected.

"Melissa?" Vichna asked hesitantly. "Just what exactly are you?"

The hologram gave that smile again even as the generator whirred to a halt, causing Harvey's image to fade to nothing. "Isn't it obvious?" As the hologram vanished, the voice shifted. Instead of coming from the generator, it seemed to come from all around, echoing throughout the entire room. "I am the Void."

Deck managed to get out a slightly panicked "What? What does that mean?" before the generator turned itself back on. For a few seconds, Vichna felt relief, thinking that whatever had just happened was a glitch and didn't mean anything. But the image over the generator was no longer the holographic Captain Harvey. Instead, it appeared to be a live feed of the *Contra Besta*'s bridge with Gregs sitting at the controls, his face utterly perplexed.

"Hey everyone?" Gregs asked. "All your video feeds to the ship just cut out. What's happening in there?"

"Gregs? Something's wrong," Captain Lersson said. "We're going back. Make sure the ship is ready to disengage as soon as the airlock door closes."

"No, we can't!" Vichna yelled. "Whatever's going on, I'm sure it's not…"

"Captain Lersson?" Gregs asked. "Professor Lashke? Can anyone in there hear me?"

"Crap," the captain said. "We can hear him but he can't hear us. That's it. We're aborting this mission, and I don't care what you say, professor. This is…"

The yellow light from inside the *Contra Besta* started flashing as the door began to close.

"No! Everyone, run!" the captain screamed. Vichna still felt a desire to argue, but the sudden turn from calm to chaos was too much, and she did what she was told. All of them bolted for the door, except they had come just far enough across the room that she saw none of them were going to make it. Captain Lersson reached it just as the door hissed, denoting that it had now sealed air-tight. The captain pounded a couple of times on the door, for all the good that would do them.

"Gregs, open the door back up! We're still in the Void! Gregs!" Vichna turned back to look at the display, hoping she would see Gregs preparing to open the door again. Instead, the view had filled with a hazy yellow color. At first she thought something was wrong with the hard-light generator. Then she realized that was just the current color of the air inside the *Contra Besta*.

"Look!" she said. Everyone came back to the generator and watched helplessly as Gregs, apparently unaware that anything was wrong with the environment, frantically tried to get back into contact with them.

"Oh dear spirits," Deck whispered. "I know that color. I know what that means."

Vichna did too, at least academically. Unlike Deck, she had never actually seen it with her own eyes, but she'd heard enough accounts of the worst parts of the Violet and Lily Wars to know Enzight gas when she saw it.

"Please tell me that's not what I think it is," the captain said. No one responded.

It was impossible to tell where exactly the gas was coming from given their current view of the bridge. Vichna had to assume that it was from somewhere that connected to the Void, although she didn't know enough about ships to figure out how that might work. It must have been coming from somewhere close to the camera because they all could clearly see the yellow fog before Gregs apparently could. There were several more seconds of him frantically working the controls before his first cough. With that, he finally looked up and saw the haze descending on him. If he understood what it was, he didn't give any indication. He spent his last moments looking utterly confused.

Vichna didn't know until later that she was the only one who watched it all the way to the end. Deck was apparently the first to look away. He would say that he had already seen enough Enzight gas victims in his lifetime, and he had never had a desire to see another, especially someone that he considered a friend. Merton claimed he was next, then Lussa. Captain Lersson watched as long as they could, saying they felt they had a duty to understand what was happening, but even they couldn't watch the whole thing. Vichna would claim that she didn't either, but she did. Her eyes never left the display no matter how much she wanted to look away. As horrifying as the scene was, it was also morbidly fascinating. Captain Harvey had created this gas. She had caused this much pain and anguish on purpose.

It started with Gregs' one cough, although it quickly became more of a hack, then a wheeze. After only a few seconds, it was evident that he couldn't breathe through the coughing fit. His face started to turn blue, then a disturbing shade of purple. At this point, Vichna wondered how he could still be alive, except he hadn't even hit the second stage yet. That came when his eyes, wide open and bloodshot, started to bleed from the tear ducts. He managed another cough, this one sending up blood right along with something darker and thicker. Vichna only saw it for a second before it fell out of view, but she thought it might be a piece of his lungs. She thought that would be the worst of it, but then the final phase started. As he continued coughing and convulsing, his entire body looked like it was shifting under his clothing. The muscle structure bulged in some places and the bones receded in others. It gave the impression for a moment that some kind of transformation was taking place. The shifting in his face, however, made it look like it was melting, his nose and cheeks and mouth sliding slowly down his skull even as the skin puffed to grotesque proportions, finally splitting from the pressure. Instead of leaking or spraying blood everywhere, though, his face and hands oozed a thick ichor that shifted in color as Vichna watched from dull brown to black to a brackish green.

And for that whole time Gregs was still alive, coughing so hard and fast that he couldn't scream at the agony.

Only twenty or so seconds after it started, Gregs was completely unrecognizable, an oozing mass of flesh only held in a vaguely human shape by his gore-covered clothing. Finally, the coughing stopped. Vichna thought it was over then, yet the putrid mass still pulsed. It took her a moment to understand that was Gregs still breathing. She didn't see the exact moment he died, though, because that was when the bloated body finally slipped from his chair and out of sight of the camera.

Vichna looked away from the display. Deck, Lussa, and the captain were all crying, the latter of whom was also on their knees, their helmet off to puke on the floor. Merton had held it together better than the others, but even he was hunched over, his hands on his knees and clearly dazed by what he had just seen. Vichna herself felt the contents of her stomach trying to come back up, an urge she desperately fought and only barely won. It was for this reason that she was the first to hear the deep rumble from the direction of the door. For a second, she thought it was about to open again and she had a moment of panic, thinking the gas in the ship would get them, before she remembered that the survival suits would protect them.

"What is that?" she asked. No one had to answer. The view from the hard-light generator changed, and they all turned to it to see the *Contra Besta* as seen from just outside the station. The air-tight seal around the door let go. Without a pilot, the ship gently drifted away from the Void, moving slowly but inexorably out into the nothingness of extra-galactic space.

The generator shut off again, leaving them once more in the dark. Captain Harvey's laugh echoed through the chamber before fading away.

1

The display inside Vichna's helmet ticked away the minutes that they stood there quietly, each of the crew trying to recover themselves from what had happened. It occurred to Vichna just how meaningless those minutes and seconds were here. Everything that they called "time" was measured in units based on the standards of Old Earth. A Sol standard day was how long it took the planet to rotate, a year was the time for it to journey around the sun. They still used those as basic measurements throughout the galaxy even though no one had lived on Earth for anything other than research purposes for thousands of years. Some planets could take multiple days for a full rotation, while others could go around their star in less than a month. Yet they continued to use the old standards.

It was completely meaningless here, though. Here there was no star to give meaning to the terms night and day, no orbit to create the concept of years. Here on the Void, time was meaningless, Vichna realized. And they had no way to escape.

"Okay, we need to focus," Captain Lersson said. They'd just finished cleaning out the inside of their helmet, which had taken the first splatter of vomit before they'd managed to get it off and eject the rest on the floor. Lersson was quick about this, evidently very much aware that the helmet would be the only thing keeping them alive if that same gas was released in here. "The first thing we need to figure out is what in Mephisto's name just happened here."

"Was that actually her?" Lussa asked. "It couldn't be, right?"

"Of course it isn't," Deck said. "She was annihilated right along with her armada. Everyone knows that."

"But do we really?" Merton asked. "It's not like anyone ever saw her body. How can we know if she was perhaps here the whole time?"

"The reason no one ever saw her body is because it was vaporized by Higgs beams just like everything else," Deck said.

"There wouldn't have been anything left to see."

"Exactly," Merton said. "So it's fully possible she escaped and faked her own death."

"That's been suggested numerous times over the last two centuries, but it just wouldn't make sense," Vichna said. "If she had lived, she would have made herself known at some point. That's just the way she was. She'd want to rub it in everyone's faces that they missed her. And also, the Captain Harvey we just saw wasn't aged a day. Two hundred years may mean little to us these days, but remember that she shunned the use of gene treatments for everything, even aging. If she were somehow still alive, she would look ancient to us."

"What then?" the captain asked. "Was that an AI? Because I sure as crap doubt it was just some kind of virtual simulation."

"But she couldn't have put an AI here," Vichna said. "The Collective would have prevented it."

"You yourself said she was in contact with them," Deck said. "Maybe they granted her some kind of exception. Or it could be that this is, in fact, one of the AIs from the Collective that's just taking her shape."

"Or maybe the Void escaped their notice," Lussa said. "Nobody else ever knew about it, so it could be that the Collective never found out, either."

Something suddenly occurred to Vichna, and if she hadn't been wearing her helmet she would have given herself a facepalm. "Maybe this isn't something we should be discussing out loud."

"Why not?" Merton asked.

"Because whether it's the real Captain Harvey or an AI or something else completely different, she's likely listening in on us right now."

They all paused, unsure of how to continue. Deck held up a finger in a wait-a-second gesture and began to fiddle with the controls on the side of his helmet. Once he seemed satisfied, he spoke again, although none of them heard his voice. They could see his lips moving through the faceplate, but he'd adjusted the settings so it didn't let any sound out. Instead a message appeared on each of their helmets' displays.

"Switch to mid-gamma transmissions. That method of communicating wasn't invented until several years after the wars."

Everyone else adjusted their helmets accordingly. Vichna hesitated but eventually followed along. There was actually a reason mid-gamma had never been used before the war. It was damaging to the human body, with prolonged exposure to it causing cellular decay. It wasn't until after genetic and gender treatments became a common part of society, soon after the wars were over, that people realized they no longer had to worry about the complications. The crew could use mid-gamma now, but it put a timer hanging over all of them. In about sixteen hours, the cellular decay would reach fatal levels unless they each had treatments to stop the effects. All the equipment they needed for that would be back on the *Contra Besta*, and she doubted they would find anything needed for treatments here on the Void. She supposed they didn't have any choice, though. If they couldn't talk and plan in secret, they might very well end up exactly like poor Gregs.

"Look at the floor as much as possible when you talk," Vichna said. "She might not be able to hear us this way, but she's probably got eyes all over the place. We don't want her to be able to read our lips."

A message popped up from Merton. "I personally don't care one way or the other who or what did this. All I want to do is get out of here alive."

"And if possible, blow this place to pieces on the way out," Deck added.

"How are we going to do that?" Lussa asked. "Our only way off the station is now floating in space and filled with deadly gas."

"Deadly to you four. Not to me," Merton said.

"What do you mean?" Lussa asked.

Vichna was confused at first until she remembered exactly how Captain Harvey's infamous doomsday weapon actually worked. "Enzight gas targets the enzymes left in a body after any gene or gender treatments. It causes everything in the body to rewrite on a genetic scale into gibberish. But Bas here has never undergone anything like that, right? So he's immune."

"You're positive?" the captain asked.

"Absolutely," Vichna said. "There's documented accounts of Harvey using the gas on her own followers to weed out anyone she considered undesirable."

"That's horrible," the captain said. "But we might be able to use this if she tries using the gas again. Otherwise, all of us need to stay in our suits unless it's absolutely necessary."

"So that takes care of how we might deal with the gas once we get back to the ship," Deck said. "Except there's still no way to reach it."

"I think there is," Vichna said. "The escape pods. We saw them on our approach. They wouldn't get us back to civilization, but we'd survive long enough to reach the *Contra Besta*."

"And you're not going to try to stop us?" Merton asked.

"Why would I do that?"

"This is your life's work or something, isn't it? I'd half expect you to keep us here as long as possible just so you can continue exploring your precious find."

"Are you kidding me? You must watch too many holothrillers. None of you have to convince me anymore. Whether that's the real Captain Harvey or an AI or something else, she's close enough to the historic Harvey that she needs to be removed. That's more important than any lost artifacts we might find here."

"Then are we in agreement?" the captain asked. "We're all getting out of here as soon as possible, and the escape pods are the best chance to do that?"

"I'm sure not going to argue with that," Lussa said.

"Me neither," Deck said.

"The escape pods are still a problem, though," Vichna said. "Did anybody bother to download the scan of the Void's outside that showed us where they were?"

"Right here," Captain Lersson said. They sent the data to each of the other suits, allowing a two-dimensional look at the Void to appear on the inside of each of their faceplates.

"The first problem is that we're not actually sure those are escape pods," Vichna said. "They certainly looked like it, but we might get to one and find they're something different entirely."

"Still better than standing around waiting for a hologram to gas us," Deck said.

"The second problem is that we don't know how to get there. We know all their locations from the outside, but the inside is a different matter entirely. We have no idea if there are straight paths to them or if the halls wind halfway around the station first. I mean, at this point we can't even be sure it has halls."

"I don't suppose there's any way for us to somehow access the computers in the Void and see if they have maps?" Merton asked.

"Normally, I'd say yes, but..." She tilted her head in the direction of the hard-light generator. That would have been how they accessed any information they needed, but now they all kept a paranoid distance from it. Theoretically, there wasn't anything that a generation-two generator could do to hurt them, and it wasn't like the representation of Captain Harvey only existed in that one spot. If it was a real person projecting their image then they would be in some kind of communications room somewhere, and if it was an AI, it might as well just be considered the whole station. Given what Harvey had said just before vanishing, Vichna was leaning more and more to the latter possibility. Either way, the generator itself should be harmless, yet it was useless for their needs as long as this other entity was in play.

"At the very least, we can designate one of the pods as our destination and use the directional navigation in our suits to head in that general direction," Deck said.

"That sounds like as solid of a plan as we're going to get," Lersson said. "Let's get moving. Remember that we're on a time limit now."

8

The first thing they had to do, a task that was more difficult than they had anticipated, was to get out of this room. A cursory check of the room didn't reveal any doors at first, other than the one they had used to come in. While the other crew members wandered around rapping on the walls or searching for some kind of control panel, Vichna stood closer to the middle and the hard-light generator, trying to think through the situation logically. Before they could determine where an exit might be, Vichna realized they should first figure out what the room's purpose was. Obviously, it was the main entrance, a sort of crazy deep-space pirate station version of a foyer. But why dedicate so much space for so little? Other than the generator, there wasn't anything of interest here.

Vichna ventured closer to the generator again. Being in the center of the room, if forced anyone who entered to approach it. Maybe that was the only reason for the room. Come in and confront the image of the notorious fallen pirate queen. It was possible that was the only way to go forward, as well.

"Vichna, are you sure you want to get that close to that thing again?" Lussa messaged to her. Outside of bed and heavily armed, she no longer seemed so child-like. Instead, she had the demeanor of a fierce lion mother ready to pounce on something dangerous approaching her cub.

"It's fine," Vichna said. "If she'd wanted to hurt us more and was capable of it, I think she would have done so by now. I just want to see if there's some way out through her."

Lussa blew her a kiss. Then she returned to searching the walls, occasionally looking back over her shoulder to make sure Vichna was still there.

"I see that you two are more than just crewmates," Harvey's voice said from behind her.

Vichna turned around the see the hologram of Melissa Harvey once more standing before her, although this time she wasn't on the hard-light generator. She stood directly to the side, as if deliberately mocking its attempts to contain her.

"Is this what you do?" Vichna asked. "Appear only before you're about to kill someone?"

Harvey waved a dismissive hand in the air. "I don't have to appear to anyone just to kill them. You don't have to worry about that. Not that I don't intend to kill you. None of your people are getting off this station intact. But please at least give me the credit of having some imagination. I'm not going to kill any of you the same way."

Vichna knew the words should have made her recoil. She'd already seen that it wasn't an empty threat. And yet that fascination from earlier returned. She was talking to history. Whoever or whatever this thing she was talking to really happened to be, it was still a piece of Captain Melissa Harvey.

Vichna looked over her shoulder at all the others. Most were too engrossed in their search to notice the hologram was back. Lussa was the only one who gave them any attention, occasionally flashing Vichna a worried look. When Vichna turned back to Harvey, the hologram was poking the air in front of her as though she were surprised she could move this far from the generator.

"Is that something you even have? Imagination?"

"Is that your way of asking what exactly I am, Professor Lashke?"

"You already know it's a question on our minds. I'm sure you were listening."

"You too would have trouble *not* listening if people were holding a conversation while standing inside you. Although I have to admit the trick you pulled afterward was pretty clever."

"So are you going to answer the question or are you going to just keep toying with me?"

"A little of both. Am I Captain Harvey or am I an AI mimicking her? Unfortunately, I can't tell you one or the other, since it's a little more complicated than that."

"Are you going to explain what that means?"

"No. It's a surprise." In a bizarrely child-like gesture, the hologram turned away from Vichna long enough to do a cartwheel.

"How are you even doing that?" Vichna asked. "A second-gen hard-light hologram shouldn't be able to leave the generator."

Harvey waved a finger at her and made a tsk-tsk noise. "Now, now. If you want to survive for more than a few minutes in the Void, let me give you this piece of advice: don't make assumptions about what kind of technology I had when I built this place."

"So now you've decided to help us? Pardon me if I have trouble believing that after you've already killed a member of our crew."

"Oh, I'm not exactly trying to help you. I've been out here alone for a very long time. I'm just trying to maximize the time I have to play with you before you get worn out from our games. If you get any help, it'll be from the other one."

"Other one? What other one?"

Harvey responded by turning an imaginary key in front of her lips.

"So is that your whole plan and purpose here?" Vichna asked. "Just to toy with us because you're bored?"

"Well, yes. That, and of course I have to kill you all eventually because you're abominations."

"Excuse me?"

"Take that one, for example." Harvey pointed to a far corner where Captain Lersson was investigating a panel in the wall. "What the hell is that even supposed to be?"

"That's the captain."

"That much information I was already able to steal from your ship's computer while it was docked, right along with your names. But that doesn't answer my question. What is it?"

Vichna bristled as she understood what Harvey was asking. "The captain comes from the Brecca province on Third Australia. The people there don't usually present as any gender at all. They use gender treatments to reach a midway point as a rite of passage when they become adults. They only become male or female long enough to mate and reproduce."

Harvey's face was an equal mix of disgust, horror, and fascination. "That's what I mean. That's not the natural order. It's a perversion of the technology I created. And from what I can tell, all but the one you call Bas Merton have engaged in it. Maybe I'll let him live for that. Or maybe I'll still kill him just for associating with you."

"Are you really so sure you can accomplish that?" Vichna asked. "For all you know, we might prove resourceful enough to escape from here alive."

"You just keep thinking that, sweetie. It will be fun watching you try. And I'll tell you what. Just to show you that I'm willing to give you a sporting chance, I'll let you out of this room. Don't expect me to give you a map of the station or anything, though. That would make things a little too easy. I'll be watching you."

Harvey's hologram winked at her and then vanished.

"Hey, I think I found the way out," the captain yelled. Vichna looked back to see that the wall had slid open next to them.

"What did you do?" Merton asked as he ran up to join them. The rest of the crew, Vichna included, was close behind.

"I don't know," the captain said. "I was just poking this metal square on the wall and it opened up. I must have accidentally entered a code or something."

Vichna was about to say that it had been Harvey that opened it, but something made her stop. Other than Lussa, none of the others had noticed her talking to Harvey again, and none of them showed any particular inclination to know what she had been doing. She looked again at Lussa, who was still giving Vichna a worried glare but wasn't otherwise talking. Vichna felt a sudden, strong sense of paranoia about what everyone else might do if they found out that Harvey had been the one to open the way. Of course, didn't the others have a right to know about some of the threats Harvey had just made? Just as soon as the question popped into her head, she pushed it away. Harvey had been light on details when it came to any upcoming danger. They all already knew that they were likely heading toward more threats, and nothing Vichna could tell them now would help or hurt them.

Still, she continued to struggle, trying to find a compelling reason to tell them all what she had just heard, but every reason evaporated before it could fully form in her mind. She finally stopped worrying about it altogether when they went through the door and into the pitch black hallway beyond.

9

Using what little light and night vision their suits could provide, they could see that the hallway was non-descript in every way – average height and gray walls stretching out far ahead of them. Periodically, the walls were interrupted by doors, all of which were shut against them. The power to the doors was off, but at each one along the way, they fumbled around the edges until they found manual-release panels. In the rooms beyond, they found absolutely nothing useful except for the knowledge that the Void had once been intended as the home to a wide variety of mundane activities. They found bathrooms, storage closets, even cleaning supplies that looked like they had never been opened or used. The majority of the rooms were completely unfurnished, but looked like they had been intended as offices. For all her studying on Captain Harvey and the Violet and Lily Wars, that was a detail Vichna had never taken the time to consider: Captain Harvey, Pirate Queen of Deep Space, had been the head of a vast and terrible organization. And like any organization, she had needed administration. Apparently, there were white collar job opportunities in genocide. But whatever bureaucracy she had intended to set up within these walls, she had been defeated before she could get very far.

"This is a whole lot different than I was expecting of this place," Deck messaged as they came out of yet another empty office. It seemed futile to continue searching them, especially since the hall and its multitude of doors continued to stretch far ahead of them, but since they didn't know anything more than the general direction they wanted to go, they still figured it was best to be thorough. The smallest detail might be the one that would save them.

"You were thinking that the Void would be nothing more than a massive series of torture chambers?" Vichna asked.

"Actually, yes. That's exactly what I was picturing."

Vichna shook her head. "Study enough history and you'll see

that evil is able to thrive because it's a lot more mundane than people expect. You can't just look for someone with an evil cackle."

Captain Lersson looked at her with a raised eyebrow. "Except the vicious holographic pirate that just killed our crewmate *did* have an evil cackle."

Vichna shrugged. "Once in a great while stereotypes are there for a reason."

Mindful that their communications method kept them on a time limit, they opened each door only long enough to see that it was of no use to them and then moved on. After about twenty doors, the offices vanished in favor of quarters that were obviously intended for living. This first became evident when they found a room with several recliners along the walls and a strange table in the center covered in some kind of green material.

"What the hell is that?" Merton asked. It seemed familiar to Vichna, but she couldn't quite recall its name. She knew it was part of some archaic game, one that had been out of fashion even before Harvey's time, but beyond that she wasn't sure. Surprisingly, it was Lussa who knew the answer.

"It's a pool table. You put balls on it and use sticks to hit them into the holes around the outside."

"How do you know that?" Lersson asked.

"I was part of a club at university," Lussa said. "We revived and played old forgotten games."

"But why would Harvey have one?" Deck asked.

"Actually, it makes sense," Vichna responded. "The whole point of this place was to preserve the arts and achievements of what Harvey considered a less-contaminated age. This must have been some kind of recreation room. She would have wanted to fill it with things she thought of as more pure."

"What does a green table have to do with gene and gender treatments, though?" Captain Lersson asked.

"Who knows," Vichna said. "Her mind worked on an entirely different wavelength than most people's."

There were a few other rooms that looked like they were for entertainment or relaxation purposes, including one that looked suspiciously like its sole purpose was for massages. Beyond this, they began to see individual quarters complete with perfectly made beds that looked like they had never been slept in. By this point, they were all getting annoyed at their lack of progress and weren't checking the rooms with the same thoroughness as before. They were just about to close the door on yet another bedroom when Vichna realized something was off and stopped them.

"What is it?" the captain asked.

Vichna stood in the doorway trying to figure out what she had subconsciously caught. All the other bedrooms were so relentlessly the same that any small detail could have seemed important. She moved into the room all the way and inspected the bed.

"This one's been slept in," she said. She pointed at the corners of the sheets. "See? Whoever made it wasn't making an effort to be thorough."

"That's hardly reliable evidence," Deck said.

It wasn't the only proof that the Void had been inhabited at one point, however. Other beds in subsequent rooms hadn't been made at all, although from the dust it was evident that they had still been abandoned some time ago.

Near the end of the hall they found the first dead body.

Ahead in the distant gloom, they could see the hall stop at what might have been a large door. From Vichna's best guess, she thought the dead person might have been running from it. The lack of bacteria or pests on the station had led to the body mummifying rather than decaying, making it remarkably easy to see the cause of death. The person, probably a woman, was in some kind of jumpsuit or uniform. Vichna saw plenty of similarities to the clothing Harvey's followers had been known to wear, although there were still plenty of differences. One of the person's arms had been cleanly severed at the shoulder, with the cloth burned around the hole suggesting some kind of laser. There wasn't any dried blood visible, leading Vichna to think that whatever had caused this had also cauterized the wound. There was another charred hole clear through from the person's back to stomach.

There was no sign around them of the woman's missing arm.

"What does this mean?" Lussa asked. "Did someone else discover the Void before we did?"

"I don't think so," Vichna said. "I think she was one of the people Harvey intended to crew the station." It seemed that her original worries of feral inhabitants had been based in some level of truth.

"Does this mean there really are people here?" Deck asked.

Vichna shook her head. "This woman has been dead for a very long time. It's probably a safe assumption that everyone else is gone as well."

"We shouldn't assume anything anymore if we want to stay alive," the captain said.

Vichna noticed that Lussa looked more troubled than the others. "What is it?"

Lussa paused like she wasn't sure if she should say anything, then pointed at the laser wounds. "Who or what do you think did that?"

"Obviously a laser weapon of some kind," Vichna said. "I'm not a weapons expert, but the burn patterns seem consistent with what I know of weapons from that time."

"Okay, sure," Lussa said. "But why?"

"What do you mean?" Merton asked.

Even as Lussa started to explain, Vichna understood the problem. There was no reason one of Harvey's own followers should have died violently on a secret space station they controlled. And they hadn't found any evidence so far that any hostile force had ever found the Void.

"Some kind of internal conflict?" the captain asked.

"Must have been," Vichna said.

"Does it really matter?" Deck asked. "Any infighting between the acolytes wiped them out long ago. Yay for us."

That seemed logical, but Vichna committed all the details to memory. There was always the possibility that any little clue could save their lives. And the missing arm bothered her. Either someone had walked away with it or it wasn't nearby, implying the woman had gone some distance before falling over dead.

Any hope that the body was an isolated incident faded as they reached the end of the hallway and its large door. There was another dead person, but this one wasn't on the floor. Instead, it had been impaled to the wall next to the door with some kind of rivet gun. This one was missing a leg below the knee and half of its face, with black scorch marks framing the empty place where it should have had a left eye and cheek bone. A partial message had been scratched into the wall on the opposite side of the door:

ENEMY BE

There was no indication if this was supposed to be the whole of the message or if the carver had been forced to leave before they were finished.

"So someone did, in fact, invade the Void," Lersson said.

"You were the one who was just saying not to assume," Vichna said. "We don't have anywhere near enough information to make educated guesses about what happened here."

"Well here's an assumption I think it's safe to make," Deck said. "It would be very stupid for us to try going through that door."

There was a long, awkward pause as they evaluated the truth of this statement. The problem was that it didn't matter what would be smart or stupid. There hadn't been any other visible path they could take. Vichna brought up the image of the outside of the Void and then added their assumed position into it. They were, in fact, heading in the general direction of several escape pods, although they also seemed to be moving slightly deeper into the station's bowels. Maybe there had been another way through somewhere behind them. In fact, Vichna was pretty sure there must have been a way that they were missing, unless the Void had been designed by a mad person.

Which, she realized, was entirely possible.

Lussa was the one who finally said the obvious. "We're going to try going through that door, aren't we?"

"Trust me, I'm willing to let anyone with a better and practical idea say so right now," the captain said. Nobody else spoke. "Then I guess we're going in." Lersson held their rifle at the ready and checked its power cells for a full charge. Everyone else did the same with their own weapons, including Vichna. Even with her general distaste for guns, she knew better than to walk into a place surrounded by corpses without her pistol ready.

56

"Okay, so we're ready to commit suicide," Merton said. "How do we open the door? I don't see a manual-release like the others."

Vichna half-expected the door to open by itself at his words, but if Harvey's hologram was listening, it didn't feel like being so obvious this time. Instead, they searched all around the immediate vicinity of the door, finding nothing. It wasn't until Lussa checked the corpse nailed to the wall that they realized there was something behind its back. It took all five of them the better part of twenty minutes to peel the desiccated husk from its resting place and drop it to the floor, although Lussa refused to actually drop it and instead set it gently to the side. While the others set about trying to open the manual-release hatch that the body had been hiding, Lussa knelt next to the body, put her right hand palm down about twenty centimeters over the forehead, and the other palm up over her own. She muttered something that sounded to Vichna like a prayer, then stood up again. As Captain Lersson got the hatch open and studied the mechanism inside, Vichna joined Lussa standing over the body.

"Mutaban Prayer for the Dead?" Vichna asked. Modern theology wasn't her strong suit, but Mutaba was a common enough religious practice in her native section of the galaxy that she recognized it.

"Yes," Lussa said simply. Her tone made Vichna think she didn't want to talk about it, but Vichna couldn't suppress her overwhelming curiosity. They had been sleeping together since early in the mission, yet Vichna had never suspected.

"I didn't know you were religious," Vichna said.

"I wouldn't say that I am. It was just the respectful thing to do."

"Why didn't you do it for the other body? Or Gregs, for that matter?"

Lussa flinched at the mention of Gregs. "There was no body for me to pray over with Gregs. And that woman back there was already on the ground. Her essence already knew which way to go. This one was upright, probably for hundreds of years. Its essence might have been lost. I was trying to help it find its way."

"Even though this person was one of Harvey's acolytes?

Probably partially responsible for the death of millions?"

"They still had an essence. It was still probably lost. I could still pray. Anything else would have been disrespectful."

Vichna got the impression that Lussa would consider any more questioning on the matter rude, so she just nodded quietly. But it was an unexpected wrinkle in Lussa's personality that Vichna hadn't suspected. Even though Vichna avoided religion herself, she found this new fact endearing. Assuming they made it back out of the Void alive, Vichna found herself wanting to stay with her and learn more, propriety be damned.

"Okay, I think we have it," the captain said. They had their head inside the hatch for the manual-release lever. "Everyone be prepared for whatever might come through that door."

They all took one last moment to make sure their weapons were ready, as well as taking care to check all the seals on their suits in case there was another gas attack. Finally, the captain turned the lever and jumped back away from the door. Everyone else aimed as the door slowly ground open, fully prepared to shoot anything that came at them.

The door opened about halfway before it stopped. It was just enough that they could all squeeze through one by one, but not enough to give them more than the tiniest glimpse of what might be in the room beyond.

"Isn't there any way for it to open more?" Merton asked.

Captain Lersson shook their head. "The mechanism looks like someone tried to intentionally sabotage it. They didn't do a very good job, and it's covered in what looks like dried blood, but this is the best I can do."

"That certainly paints a cheery picture," Deck messaged.

Everyone went quiet. Vichna could only assume they were all asking themselves the same question she was:

Which of them was going to go first?

10

Captain Lersson went first.

They finally said it was the only option that made sense, being the captain. Vichna wasn't sure that a captain's duty to their crew still counted when the ship was no longer in the picture, but everyone else looked relieved that someone else was going to take responsibility. Lersson stood at the narrow opening, shining their light into the room beyond, hoping they could get some idea of what threats might be on the other side.

"It just looks like another huge room," Lersson said.

"No details?" Vichna asked.

"Not that I can see. It's not quite as large as the first one we were in, but from what I can see of the walls, they look blank. No furniture or fixtures... wait. There's... damn it."

"What?" everyone messaged at once.

"Take a look." The captain stepped aside, allowing Vichna a narrow view of the room beyond. Their description was accurate, but there was, in fact, one notable feature in the room, even if it was hidden by the gloom: another hard-light generator. It blinked on for just a second, long enough for Harvey's hologram to give her a wink and a wave, then vanished.

Vichna stepped away so the others could see what had worried them. Deck cursed the loudest and in the most languages. "We can pretty much guarantee that we'll be watched in there. And that it's a trap."

Merton snorted. "I think the first clue to that was the dead body and the warning about an enemy."

Something about what he'd just said disturbed Vichna, but she couldn't quite put her finger on it. She didn't have the time to think it through, either, as Lersson gently pushed her aside and positioned themself at the door again.

"Okay, so if we're going to do this..." they said. Nobody wished them good luck. Personally, Vichna didn't think luck would have much to do with them surviving whatever they were about to face. It would probably rely a little on skill and a lot of the whims of Harvey's avatar.

With the rifle in front of them and their light on the ground to search for possible booby traps, Lersson squeezed through the door and paused just inside the room. After a few seconds, they went in farther and just out of the limited visual field the others had through the stuck door.

"Captain?" Deck asked. "Keep communicating with us."

"Nothing out of the ordinary yet," Lersson said. "Unless... wait..." There was a long pause before the captain messaged again. "I found the woman's arm. Well, I'm assuming I did. It's got to be one of these arms."

With that ominous note, Captain Lersson went silent again for nearly a minute before continuing. "I'm not seeing anything that looks dangerous, although I'm guessing from all the bodies that we still need to worry. Everyone come in one by one. Slowly. Don't step in anybody."

Lussa went next, followed by Deck, Vichna, and Merton guarding the rear. The two security personnel had trouble squeezing through with their exoskeletons, and there was some concern for a moment that they would need to leave them behind. However, they were both eventually able to shove themselves through with only minor scratches, leaving them all inside the room. The first things Vichna noticed upon entering were the heaped shapes on the floor just beyond what they'd been able to see from the outside. From just a cursory glance, Vichna could tell that they all seemed to match the bodies outside, both in clothing and level of decomposition. Just as Lersson had said, there was a severed arm close to the door, and just beyond there were a number of body parts that had come from at least two different people. Nobody wanted to spend much time examining any of it, but a quick look showed similar burn marks on every corpse.

"Does anyone see a weapon around that could have caused this?" Merton asked.

"Not that I can see," Lussa said. "Maybe that's a good thing."

Vichna didn't think so, however. If one of these people had

been the one to kill all the others, then they would have been among the bodies with the weapon nearby. The lack of a weapon implied that the killer had gotten away, or perhaps wasn't a person at all. Vichna's earlier sense that something was off came back to her, but she dismissed it. *Everything* was off about this situation, after all.

"I think that might be a door over there," Deck said. He swung the light on his helmet to the far wall just beyond the hard-light generator. Sure enough, there was a closed door there, smaller and less ominous than the one they had just come through. The instinctive part of Vichna's brain took that to mean there was safety, at least temporarily, beyond it, but she wasn't sure if she completely trusted that. They had already seen plenty of features in the Void that implied its designer had known how to psychologically manipulate its inhabitants.

"It can't be that easy, can it?" Merton asked.

"I wouldn't count on it," the captain said. "Here's what we're going to do: everyone single file in the same order we came in. Try to stay at least two meters from the person in front of you in case they, and I guess by that I really mean me, set off some kind of trap. Be prepared to run for the door on my command. Everyone understand?"

They didn't even need to say anything. Instead, they all took up their positions behind Lersson and waited for them to take the lead. Lersson took a deep breath first, then carefully began walking among the bodies across the room.

Vichna felt a deep dread in the pit of her stomach with every deliberate step they took. It felt to her like they had gone too far without anything of note happening, and that just didn't work with what she knew of Harvey's personality. This was the moment where something would occur, and for every meter they walked without incident, her anxiety increased. She took a step and thought *Now's the moment where everything goes wrong*, and it wasn't. *Now*. Yet it wasn't.

Now?

She thought she saw the generator flicker ever so briefly to life. Vichna felt a powerful pull in her gut, a deep-seated need to jump, and she couldn't help herself. With a wordless cry she leapt to her right, a sudden movement that startled everyone else around her to a stop.

That was probably what kept Captain Lersson from being sliced in half.

The beam came from the ceiling, and Vichna had just enough time to realize that they'd all been so worried about potential traps along the floor that none of them had thought to look up. A blue laser lanced down at them from an angle, ripping right through the space where Lersson had been about to step. Everyone immediately scattered. Merton tried to go back, only to have another beam come down close enough that Vichna could see a small piece of exoskeleton separate from his shoulder and fall to the floor. Any attempt at order among them was now gone. Lersson screamed for them to run, not even bothering to say it through a mid-gamma transmission. Another laser hit just to the left of Lussa, and one behind Deck. That was enough to get all of them moving in a mad rush to reach the door.

Vichna looked up just as another laser fixed on Lersson. The quick flash of blue light showed her several turrets on the walls near the ceiling. There were at least two working ones that she could see, as well as a charred hole that might have once been a third. So someone at some point had tried to fight back and scored a hit. That meant that they might have a chance.

Vichna shouted and pointed, hoping anyone else would see what she was seeing. Merton seemed to notice and immediately stopped to train his weapon at the walls. That seemed suicidal to Vichna, standing still when the turrets could clearly track them, yet the next one that shot at Merton went wide, causing him to flinch yet still missing him by a decent margin. The flash it caused was enough for Merton to see its location, though, and he fired back. The room was briefly illuminated with an explosion as the turret took a direct hit and turned to slag. Vichna thought she saw several more turrets up in the corners. In fact, there were enough turrets that each member of the group could have been shot twice over in these few seconds.

Vichna stopped as she had a sudden moment of realization: there was no good reason why every single one of them shouldn't already be dead.

She stopped in the middle of the floor, very much aware of how close she was to the hard-light generator. Several more shots rained down from above, chasing the others as they went for the door. While it was possible that the lasers were missing because their targeting systems had a problem with the darkness, Vichna doubted they could be that primitive. In fact, they were acting so primitive that...

She changed the display in her helmet to look for energy signatures, allowing her to see the lines of power going to each of the turrets through the walls. In a modern weapons system, such lines would have been better shielded to protect against exactly this sort of thing. That alone was strange, given that such shielding should have been available in Harvey's time. What was even more of note, however, was the way the power to the turrets seemed to be flickering. The lines of energy pulsed as though someone were turning the power on and off. The result, apparently, was the turrets' poor aiming skills. It was as though someone was powering the turrets while someone else was trying to stop them.

Vichna had a memory of what Harvey's hologram had off-handedly said. *If you get any help, it will be from the other one.*

Her thoughts were interrupted by Lussa knocking her to the side. A split second later, a laser hit where Vichna had been. Lussa pulled her to a makeshift cover behind a couple of bodies. As protection went, it was next to nothing, considering the lasers could slice right through them, but Lussa probably figured it was better than nothing.

"What do you think you're doing, just standing in the middle of the room?" Lussa asked.

"Look at the energy signatures," Vichna replied. Lussa gave her a confused look but did what she said. After a second, comprehension shown on her face. Everyone else must have received the message, too, because as one, they turned their weapons on the turrets that they could suddenly see by the signatures. The terrified moment they'd just had vanished as quickly as it had come, as they easily shot each and every turret.

For several seconds after the shooting stopped, everyone was quiet. Deck was the first to break the silence. "What the hell was that all about?"

Vichna explained what she had seen with the pulsing energy signatures, and mentioned her theory that Harvey wasn't the only person or thing in the Void with them.

"You think we have an ally on the station somewhere?" Lersson asked.

"The evidence is starting to look that way," Vichna said.

"I don't know. It kind of seems like a leap in logic to me," Merton said.

Vichna almost said that it matched what Harvey had told her, but she felt a sudden sense of paranoia at the idea of Merton knowing she had been talking to the hologram again earlier. There was still deep sense of mistrust toward Merton and his anti-GT ways. Her conversation with Harvey was something she absolutely needed to discuss with the others, but preferably in a way that Merton wouldn't receive the transmission.

"It's a theory we should at least keep in mind," Lersson said. "Now that we're out of danger, though, we should concentrate on the next door."

Vichna nodded and approached the door first. It didn't appear to be much different than the ones they had found out in the hall. Although she knew that they should be cautious going through any door, this one obviously didn't have the psychological impact of the previous one, and she found herself instinctively trying to relax as she approached.

It was a feeling she instantly distrusted. The question from earlier still stuck in her head: why had there not been proper shielding on the turrets' power lines?

The rest of the crew approached the door behind her, with Captain Lersson at the end keeping their weapon trained on the ceiling in case there were any turrets they had all missed. In fact, Vichna realized, everyone was looking up now.

"Captain, it's my vote that we get the hell out of this room," Deck said. He opened the door's manual-release panel and pulled the lever. The door ground open, exposing a hallway beyond that was noticeably shorter than the first.

"Your vote is noted and approved," Lersson said. They lowered their weapon, no longer looking at the ceiling. Of course, they weren't looking at the floor anymore, either. None of them had been. The whole crew had been distracted by the easy-to-see power lines in the walls. Lines that, Vichna realized, had been left visible on purpose.

"Wait!" Vichna screamed. The message translated to everyone else's displays without the urgency in her voice.

The captain didn't have time to respond to her. There must have been a trigger on the floor that the rest of them had missed. Lersson, however, took a step that was accompanied by a blinding flash. Vichna couldn't even be positive what she saw, it all happened so fast. She suspected there was a new laser beam flashing at ankle level, but her eyes couldn't quite take in how quickly it flashed on and off. The whole event took only a couple of seconds.

One moment the captain had been walking toward them.

The next there was a steaming pile of meat on the floor.

Several minutes later, when they were on the other side of the door and again shell-shocked by the sudden unexpected death of a crewmate, Vichna would replay the images her suit had recorded in an effort to understand what had just happened. In slow motion, she was able to understand, even if the video again made her nauseated with the pure grotesquery of it. The laser had actually a flat beam, not ever a full meter wide, going across the room at ankle height. If anyone else had been as far back as Lersson when they triggered the trap, that person too would have been sliced to pieces in only a few blinks of the eye. The beam had cut cleanly through the captain's boots, instantly cauterizing the wound and preventing even a drop of blood from spilling. Everything above the beam had continued moving forward with the captain's momentum. As she continued viewing the video, Vichna would look for any sign that Captain Lersson understood what was happening, but there was nothing. It all happened too fast for them to feel pain. There had even been a small smile on their face, as though strangely content and happy that they had made it through the room unscathed.

Then that smile had dropped away, quite literally. In slow motion, the beam shut off, and everything above Lersson's ankles fell forward. In another instant, the beam was back, cutting cleanly through Lersson's shins. Gone and then back again, through their knees. Thighs. Groin. Stomach. Chest. A mini rainstorm of fingers on either side. Neat cross-sections of arm muscle. Pieces of organs falling out where they didn't quite burn into place. Shoulders. Neck. A severed head, almost comically suspended over the mass of charred gore beneath.

That smile had still been there.

Then the head and helmet went through the beam as well. Three neat slices. The mouth. Just below the eyes. The upper forehead.

This was the point in the recording where the beam stopped flashing. It was also the point where Vichna became aware of the hysterical screaming of her crewmates.

11

As far as any of them could tell, there was no practical reason to close the door between the turret room and the corridor beyond. Nothing indicated they would be in danger. Yet they still made the effort to find the manual door control on this side and shut it. No one wanted to see what they had left in the room behind them.

The short hall they now found themselves in was strangely formal compared to the stark utilitarianism of everything else they had seen thus far. The walls were actually painted a soothing purplish-blue color, and there were several couches against the walls. There was a desk at the far end and several more doors, yet none of the crew made the effort to go and explore them just yet. Instead, now was the moment for all of them to deal with what was happening to them.

While Vichna silently stood in a corner and reviewed the video, Merton collapsed to his knees in a fit of tears near one of the couches. Deck paced and muttered to himself, the mid-gamma transmissions broadcasting his words as nothing but a meaningless jumble of letters. Not only was he also in tears, but several times he looked like he was fighting not to puke. Lussa just stood in the middle of the hall staring into nothing, too shell-shocked to even acknowledge anything around her.

Vichna saved the video and surveyed the reactions of everyone around her. More and more, it seemed like none of them would escape the Void alive, but if they were to have any chance at all, someone needed to take the lead. If anything, she was surprised no one else had done so already. They were all military or combat trained, although Vichna supposed it had been so long since any of them actually needed to use that training that it might have gotten rusty.

So she supposed that made her the most likely candidate to take the lead, but the idea terrified her. She was used to giving lectures to thousands of people. That she knew how to do, and that was about it. Even going on the mission had challenged her comfort zone. Yet she was the one with the most knowledge regarding everything they might still face. That left her as the only logical option.

She looked over at Lussa, who was trained for these kind of situations, yet had still frozen in the face of terrors she hadn't expected. Sweet, innocent, fifty-eight-year-old Lussa. If nothing else, Vichna swore that she would get Lussa out of here alive.

"We need a plan," Vichna said. "But first we need a moment to rest."

"Rest? Seriously, rest?" Deck asked. "You have to be joking."

"We have about fourteen hours before the mid-gamma cellular breakdown becomes irreversible," Vichna said. "That's bad, but not our most pressing concern. We need to be more worried about accidentally making stupid mistakes."

"A stupid mistake?" Merton asked. "Is that what you call what just happened? You don't have any right to talk about the captain that way."

"It was a mistake on all our parts," Vichna said. "We let ourselves get complacent for just a few seconds. We should have still been checking for traps."

"So now what just happened to Mart was our faults?" Deck asked. He approached her with his fists clenched. Vichna was sure he was about to lay one across the face of her helmet, but that was when Lussa finally came out of her stupor and placed a steadying hand against Deck's chest.

"That's not what she's saying at all." Lussa turned to look at Vichna. "Right?"

Merton, too, seemed to be getting a little more control of himself. "I think what the professor is saying is that if we charge forward right now, more of the same is going to happen. We should take the time to stop and lick our wounds before trying anything else. Is that about right?"

Vichna was surprised that Merton agreed with her, but she was grateful nonetheless. "Yes. That's exactly it."

Deck took a deep breath, sniffled back some tears, and a lot of the violent tension left his body. "Okay. Fine. So what are you suggesting?"

"We thoroughly check this room first. It looks safe enough, but

I think we all know by now not to assume. If we decide it is safe, or at least safe enough, we stop to rest. I don't think any of us expected to be in here this long. We'll get a couple hours of sleep, if that's possible. Maybe eat what little we have for rations in my bag."

"And pee," Lussa said. "I've been holding it in for an hour. Frankly, I'm surprised I didn't wet myself when, well, you know." She gestured at the door they had just closed. Vichna suddenly realized that she, too, was in desperate need of a bathroom, and judging from the way Merton and Deck fidgeted, they were feeling the same need.

"Right," Vichna said. "So let's search this room. And assuming we don't find anything we need to run screaming from, we'll stop for two hours, sleep if we can, or if we can't, we'll just get off our feet. And we'll see if we can come up with a more concrete plan."

Given the fatal mistake of the last room, they all searched the current room with a thoroughness they had probably never before attempted in their life. Vichna's first guess was that this was probably intended to be some kind of receptionist area, although she wasn't sure yet why such a thing could be needed. The couches had a layer of dust on them but were otherwise in pristine condition. She was surprised to find that they appeared to be upholstered in real leather, despite the fact that such a material had been highly illegal in Harvey's heyday. Or maybe she wasn't that surprised at all. The desk looked like it had never been used. They searched all the drawers for any potential supplies yet found them completely empty. Merton did find a red button on the underside of the desk within a secretary's easy reach, yet none of them dared touch it. After that, they all gave the desk a wide berth.

They approached the three doors with a great deal of caution, although in at least two cases, their wariness was unwarranted. One of the doors led to a supply closet, although like the desk, it was completely empty of anything remotely useful. Apparently, no one had ever gotten around to stocking the Void with supplies before Harvey and her armada made their last stand. The second door, much to their relief, was a bathroom. They weren't so happy to see it, however, that they didn't check it top to bottom before any of them dared use it. It appeared safe, although it didn't have any running water. That didn't stop them from each taking a turn to remove their survival suits and relieve their bladders. The lack of water or toilet wipes, unfortunately, meant that anyone who needed to get rid of something more solid would have to hold it in for a while longer.

Once these necessary duties were taken care of, they assigned a brief period of time for sleep. Given that they still weren't completely sure the room didn't have a nasty surprise waiting for them, they all agreed that it would be best to sleep in shifts, with two of them resting for an hour while the other two kept watch, followed by them switching places. Lussa and Deck got the first sleeping shift. Despite protests from both of them that there was no way they'd be able to sleep, they passed out within minutes, leaving Vichna to keep an eye on things with Merton.

Vichna found herself staring at Lussa for several minutes, watching the way she sprawled on her couch like a cat, and smiling when she saw that the girl was drooling slightly inside her helmet. Under normal circumstances, Lussa would have been snoring softly about now, but the fine adjustments to the air from her suit somehow fixed that. It was a shame Lussa had the helmet on. Vichna would have liked to lovingly run her hands through Lussa's hair.

"I don't judge you, you know," Merton said. Vichna turned to see him sitting cross-legged on the floor in front of Deck's couch, his rifle ready in his lap.

"Judge me for what?" Vichna asked.

Merton nodded his head at Lussa. "You two. Together. I know it worries you. I see it in the way you look at her."

"It's… it's nothing," Vichna said. "Her and I, it's just a relationship of convenience."

"We both know that's not true. Everyone else on the ship knew it, too. It might have started out as two horny people looking for a warm bed, but in a short time it's become more."

Vichna frowned. "You and the rest of the crew talked about us a lot?"

"Everyone else talked. I listened."

"And what exactly did they say?"

Merton chuckled, which came across on Vichna's display as simply as *mirthful noise.* "There was a little bit of the proverbial clutching of pearls at first, I have to admit. Someone your age with someone so young? Such a scandal. They all got over it eventually."

"And that includes you?"

"I never had a problem with it to begin with. You're forgetting the culture I come from. We don't use the same treatments as the rest of you, so our view of age isn't as skewed as the rest of yours has become. To anyone else on the *Contra Besta,* Lussa was a child barely old enough to even be there. But to me, she's always been an adult. That's why I advocated so much for her to be a part of the crew when I saw what she could do despite never being in the military. And that's also why, when she decided to be with you, I saw it as a fully informed, adult decision."

Vichna wasn't sure if she wanted to continue down this line of conversation, but her curiosity got the better of her. "So you're more approving of two people so radically different in age than you are of gender treatments in general?"

"Hmph. Sounds like Lussa's been whispering about me behind my back."

"So you wouldn't say that's true?"

"This may come as a surprise to you, but where I come from, I'm considered radically progressive."

"You're right. That would be a surprise. Lussa said you were part of the Purser Sect."

"No, I was raised with the Purser Sect. That's very different."

"Yet you still don't believe in GT or any sort of genetic manipulation."

"I don't believe that it's the path for me, but it's not my right to decide whether anyone else does it. I mean, I'm here on this mission, am I not? If I were still a strict Purser, I would never have signed up with this crew, let alone joined the marines. My family considers me horribly unclean just be being around you people."

"But if you're going to go that far, why not go all the way? Why not change your gender and see what it's like?"

"Because nature made me a man, and I've never felt the desire to be anything else. Not that I don't admit to being curious." He pointed at Deck. "Deck and Gregs had, well, I wouldn't call it a relationship. They didn't care about each other quite that much. It was more of a standing agreement. Whenever either of them changed gender, they came to the other one first for what they would call 'testing their equipment.' One time, after they had both become women, they invited me to join. Now, the Pursers may have multiple hang-ups when it comes to sex and gender, but polyamory is not one of them. I joined them. And watching them enjoy themselves as women? Well, I'm not going to say there wasn't a part of me that didn't want to understand how it felt."

"But you never went through with it?"

"No. In the end, the curiosity wasn't strong enough to overpower my personal needs."

"Which are what, exactly?"

"The need to just be me, of course. I'm a man. That's how I identify. That's what I need to be. Deck and Gregs, they had a very different need. And I have no more right to interfere with that need than they do... uh, did, with mine."

"So you don't subscribe to Melissa Harvey's idea that people like us are impure?"

"No! Is that really something you were worried about?"

Vichna's cheeks grew hot. "I suppose it was."

"Let me tell you something plain and straight, Professor. Gregs and Captain were more than just crewmates. They were my friends and, yes, at one point Gregs was even my lover. If Captain Harvey miraculously showed up in the flesh in front of me, there is not a single part of me that would ever show her loyalty. There is, however, a very large part of me that would need to slaughter her in the most violent fashion possible."

Vichna knew that should have reassured her, yet somehow it didn't. For some reason she couldn't understand, his words were especially chilling, and they made her want to turn her back on him even less than before.

12

Once the hour was up, Vichna and Merton woke Lussa and Deck, then took their own places on the couches. Vichna had been just as skeptical as the others that she would be able to sleep under these circumstances, but the instant she was in a reclining position, consciousness left her. She dreamed of Harvey's hologram manifesting itself first outside the hard-light generators, then on the *Contra Besta*, and then across the galaxy. Harvey's familiar cackle accompanied the whole dream, and despite the environmental control of her survival suit, Vichna woke an hour later in a cold sweat.

They all shared what little they had for emergency rations from Vichna's supplies, each taking a turn with their helmet off so that, if something were to happen, it wouldn't hit every one of them at once. When they were finished with that, they had no choice but to face the inevitable: they needed to explore the third door by the desk.

While they'd been able to discern rather easily that the other two doors were somewhat mundane in nature, it was obvious that the same could not be said about this one. While it lacked the intentional ominousness of the door to the turret room, it had still been designed in such a way for it to suggest *this is important*. It was slightly larger and more ornate than the other two, but the most striking feature was actually what it lacked. As far as anyone could tell, there was no way to open it.

While Deck and Lussa examined the door, being very careful not to actually touch it yet, Vichna let her gaze wander around the office. The very fact that there was an office here at all still perplexed her.

"Not only does there not seem to be a manual-release," Deck said, "but the walls here are too well-shielded for me to see if there are any energy signatures going to any kind of control."

"Maybe there's supposed to be a secret knock," Lussa said.

Deck shrugged. "Hell, I would think that was a stupid

suggestion if everything else about this place weren't completely crazy. So go ahead and give it a try."

"No way. I'm not touching that thing. You're the engineer. You try it."

"Since when does engineering have anything to do with knocking on a door?"

"Maybe we're approaching this the wrong way," Vichna said. "Let's think about what purpose this room is actually supposed to serve."

"As far as I can tell, it doesn't serve any purpose," Merton said.

"Just like everything here," Deck added.

"No, I don't believe that's the right way to think of it," Vichna said. "It's easy to just try passing Harvey off as mad, but it wasn't the kind of madness that led her to do stupid things. Everything about the Void must have a reason, even if that reason only made sense to her."

"Okay," Lussa said. "If we come at it from that angle, then what's the purpose of everything we've seen so far?"

"Other than just being a bunch of murder chambers," Deck said.

"But they weren't," Vichna said. "Not all of them. Really, not even most of them. The first room was, well, I suppose the best way to describe it would be the welcoming room. Then we had a long hallway with crew quarters and administration."

"And then a murder chamber," Deck insisted.

"No, not a murder chamber. Well, okay. Yes. It was a murder chamber. But more accurately, it was a security checkpoint. A way to keep undesirables out. And then we have here, which is..." She looked around, making one last confirmation on her theory. "A receptionist's office and waiting room. So given all that and what we already know about the Void, then what conclusion does that leave us with?"

Everyone appeared to give this serious thought, but none of them came to the same conclusion as her. Vichna gave them a push. "If you ignore the odd placement of the crew and administration, which I personally think might be just because Harvey wanted them before security, then..."

Lussa interrupted her. "A museum?"

Deck looked at her. "How would you come to that conclusion?"

"Because that's what supposed to be here, isn't it?" Lussa asked. "Priceless artifacts, rare works of art, countless genetic samples. If it's everything Vichna says it is, then the collection should be amazing. And since everything we've seen so far suggests Harvey had an ego bigger than the planet Dionysus, then…"

"Wait, wait, wait," Deck said, holding up his hands. He looked around the room as though really seeing it for the first time. "You mean to tell me Harvey actually intended to bring people here and show off her loot? As in, charging admission and everything?"

"Well, I don't know about that last part, although knowing her history, I wouldn't put it past her," Vichna said. "But as for actually having the Void open for visitors? Yes, I'm beginning to think that's exactly what she had in mind."

Merton snorted. "Doesn't it defeat the purpose of putting the station at the edge of known space if she was just going to invite the entire galaxy to come see it?"

Vichna shrugged. "Judging from layout we've seen so far, I don't think she was exactly going to put a giant sign on the place and advertise for families to come spend their vacations here. The crew area would have been further out of the way, and this room probably would have been much bigger to accommodate a larger number of people. No, it looks like this would have been an invite-only situation. Sort of, 'Hey you, foreign dignitary, I want to intimidate you, so we're going to blindfold you and take you to my secret collection, and if you step out of line, you'll never leave.'"

"That's all fascinating conjecture," Merton said. "But how does this information help us get out of here?"

"For one thing, it means we probably know what's beyond this door," Vichna said.

"You think that's it?" Lussa asked. "Everything she ever raided from the entire galaxy is behind there?"

Vichna glanced again at the door. "Knowing what we do about Harvey, I'd say this door isn't dramatic enough. If I had to guess, we'll find another layer of security behind here, and *then* the treasure room."

"But again, the treasure room isn't a way out," Merton said.

"Yet it does seem like it's going to be the only way through. Even if we haven't found any sort of emergency escape pod, even if those things we saw on the outside aren't what we need at all, I refuse to believe Captain Harvey didn't have some sort of way for her to escape."

Deck paused. The flicker on the inside of his helmet told Vichna that he was checking something on his display. "That may be the case. But according to the rough map we're creating as we go along, we're heading deeper into the station rather than to the outside. Although… hmm."

"What is it?" Merton asked.

"Remember that gravitational anomaly we detected when we first entered the Void? Whatever it is, my suit is saying it's close."

"How close?" Lussa asked.

Deck pointed to the door. "I still couldn't tell you what it is, however."

Vichna nodded. "I'm guessing that would be the final level of security before the vault. If we get through that, then maybe we'll find some kind of central operations beyond. If there's not a way out there, then at the very least there should be some way to find one."

"And yet again," Deck said, "we still run into the problem of how we are supposed to get through this door right in front of us."

"Actually, no," Vichna said. "I think we already found the way through a while ago. Think about it." Vichna went over to the desk and stood behind it. "All of you standing there are, oh, let's say Merton is one of Harvey's guards while Lussa and Deck are important guests. Or more like hostages, most likely. You came in here after going through the last security checkpoint and find me, Harvey's personal secretary, waiting for you. You ask to be let in and I…" She pointed at the button they had found earlier. "…do exactly that."

"Are you sure that's something you really want to press?" Deck asked. "I mean, it's red."

"So?"

"So at no point in the history of mankind has a red button been a good thing. Green, pink, blue, maybe even yellow, sure. But a red button always means someone is about to get messed up."

"It's the only possible way in that I can see. Unless everyone else would rather continue fumbling around for another switch."

No one look particularly excited about that possibility.

"Fine then. Pressing the button seems to be the only option." Vichna reached down to touch it, yet paused. Deck was right. It really was an alarming shade of red. "Um, maybe it would be a good idea if everyone joined me behind the desk. Just in case."

"Hell, you don't need to tell me twice," Deck said. They all huddled next to her behind the desk, staying as close to the actual button as possible. Vichna took a deep, calming breath first, then pressed the button.

They all went blind.

"What the fuck?" Deck screamed. Or at least that's what she thought he screamed. The sudden, all-encompassing flash of light made it impossible to see any message transmitted to her screen. It sounded like he said it through a verbal channel, maybe, but the light was accompanied by a loud, deep thrumming noise. Their suits automatically adjusted their sound input so that the noise wouldn't do permanent damage to their ears, but even afterward, they could still feel the vibration deep within their bones. The sound petered out quickly, and their suits readjusted back to normal.

"Oh my essence, I can't see," Lussa said.

Vichna blinked, realizing that the afterimage of the initial flash was fading from her retinas to show only black beyond. She thought for a moment that she'd been rendered blind permanently, until she realized she could still see the data and the screen inside her helmet.

"Our visors went black to protect our eyes from the flash," Vichna said. "Give them a moment to adjust."

After a few seconds, the visors faded away from pure black to show them the room around them. The desk and a small area immediately around them were untouched, apparently protected by some kind of energy shield or barrier. The entire rest of the room was covered in a fine layer of dark soot. At first, Vichna was unsure where the soot had come from, until she realized that was all that remained of the room's paint job. She touched the wall, which was oddly cool, and the soot came off on her finger to show the bare metal walls beneath. The flash had vaporized everything in the room that hadn't been in their small protected zone. The couches were now neat piles of ash.

"That," Lussa said, "was probably not the right button."

There was a lot of cussing and recrimination for the next few minutes before they finally started searching the desk again. This time, they found a hidden panel next to the red button. It looked like it would have required a key, except the lock had never been installed. Inside they found another button, this one refreshingly blue. Even so, they all stood once more in the desk's safe zone before anyone would allow Vichna to press it.

This time there was an audible click as the door unlocked.

13

Without full power, the door wouldn't open by itself. All four of them had to work together to pull the door aside. They didn't discuss what they thought would be on the other side, but Vichna was sure they didn't expect what they actually saw.

"Wow," Lussa said. "What even is this?"

Those were the only words anyone said for nearly a minute as they all stared at the room beyond in utter amazement. Vichna had thought the first room they entered was big, but it was nothing compared to this place. As far as Vichna could tell, this room had to take up the vast majority of the Void as a whole, but trying to describe it even to herself took some effort. The entirety of the room was roughly equivalent to a small town on her home planet. Looking up at the very center of the roughly spherical room, there was a circular structure slightly larger than the *Contra Besta*. It was made of a gleaming white metal, with several small red protrusions that might have been doors. Vichna's first impression was to say it was floating, but as she tried to make sense of the rest of the room, she realized that wasn't the best way to describe it. Maybe it was hanging from above, maybe something was holding it up from below. It was difficult to say, since the entire cavernous room had no concept of up or down.

Radiating out from the white sphere at the center and criss-crossing throughout the entire cavern were an uncountable number of stairs and walkways. From Vichna's current vantage point, some were upside-down, some were sideways. Some seemed to deny not just physics but logic itself when stairways appeared to lead up into their own bottom. One catwalk went straight up some thirty meters to their left, ending in a wall for no apparent reason. The entire thing was a geometrical nightmare that made Vichna's head hurt.

Mindful of the possibility of more traps, the four of them carefully stepped through the doorway to the platform beyond. The platform was roughly triangular, and large enough to hold perhaps twenty people at a time. Each of the three points offered a separate path deeper into the cavern. To their right, there were stairs going down, curving at an angle that no one should have been able to stand on before disappearing somewhere below them. She would have said they disappeared into the dark, but the cavern seemed to have its own weather system with occasional hazy wisps of clouds, sometimes even giving off sparks of lightning in the direction of the central white sphere. To their left was another staircase, this one going up and taking a sharp angle so the stairs were on their side and curving back over their heads twenty meters up. Directly in front of them was a sturdy-looking bridge with railings, gently sloping upward until it went directly into one of the red nodes on the sphere.

The only other thing on the platform with them was another hard-light generator.

"Any ideas, Professor?" Merton asked. He said it through a vocal channel. Vichna had to admit it was getting a bit annoying having to read everyone's speech instead of hearing it, and she switched to an audible communication.

"If I was forced to guess, I'd say that's the vault," Vichna said, pointing at the central sphere. "Everything else, well, I suppose it's probably the final level of security."

"Why would anyone build anything like this?" Lussa asked.

"Because why wouldn't I?"

The generator came alive and Harvey's hologram appeared, a jaunty cock to her hip and a bizarrely giddy smile on her face. "I mean seriously, if you had the money and technology to create an Escher room, wouldn't you?"

"An Escher room?" Merton asked.

"I think she's referring to an ancient Earth artist, but I can't be sure," Vichna said. "I know history well enough, but art history is just outside my expertise. And I honestly couldn't tell you what he has to do with this nightmare."

Harvey pouted. "You know, it's not as fun showing off my knowledge if you don't even get my references."

Merton walked up to the walkway going straight up into the sphere. "This looks way too easy. I'm not setting foot on this thing."

"Are you sure?" Harvey asked. "Don't you at least want to see what would happen?"

All four of them responded at once. "No."

Harvey grinned. "Ha! I guess my counterpart has done a little too good of a job. Fine. I'll tell you this one for free, since it would already be part of the programmed security protocols and neither of us would actually be doing this. You triggered the flash attack in the previous room, so if you try to walk on it, the walkway will vanish halfway through."

"Vanish?" Vichna asked. "How could it simply vanish if we're already walking on it?"

"It's hard-light generation four," Harvey said. Her image flickered. "I told you before not to assume what kind of technology I have."

Merton turned to Vichna. "I thought you said there was no way she could have anything beyond generation two?"

"And what does she mean by counterpart?" Deck asked. "Please tell me there's not more than one of her."

"I don't know," Vichna said. "I haven't figured any of this out yet for sure. But it looks like if we want to go any farther, we have to go through..." She pointed at the maze of stairs, walkways, and generally unidentifiable structures in the cavern around them. "...that."

"This whole place is just bad design," Deck said, blowing out a heavy sigh.

"Bad design, or best design?" Harvey asked. As the others moved closer to the stairs on their right to get a better view, Harvey's image flickered again. Vichna stayed back to continue examining the generator.

"You're not as strong as you're trying to have us believe," Vichna said, directing her words through a channel meant solely for Harvey's hologram.

"Oh really? And what makes you say that?"

"You've been flickering. Something in the technology is failing. It's not as advanced as you would have us think."

"Oh wow, that's rich," Harvey said. "There's going to be a point in the future where I'm going to remind you that you said that." The hologram vanished. Vichna stayed at the generator, inspecting it to see if she could see any obvious flaws, but while she knew the history of such technology fairly well, the inner workings were still a mystery to her.

"Are you coming or are you going to just keep staring at that thing until we all die?" Deck asked her, once again switching back to mid-gamma transmissions. Realizing there was probably nothing more she could learn here, Vichna went to join the rest of them in inspecting the stairs.

"I'm not so sure if it's a good idea for all of us to use the same staircase," Merton said.

"I'm not so sure if it's a good idea for us to use either staircase," Lussa said, pointing to the place where the stairs started to curve at what seemed an impossible angle. "We're not going to be able to walk on these for long before we fall."

"No, you're making assumptions based on our normal idea of gravity," Vichna said. "If this cavern were on one of our home planets, then yes, of course we would fall. And we're so used to artificial gravity in the floors of our ships that we almost assume it's universal. But look." With careful movements, she went down about six or seven steps, then looked back at them. At this point, the stairs had begun to curve so they looked inclined, but she didn't feel like she was about to slip. Instead, her crewmates on the platform now looked like they were leaning at a precarious angle.

"The gravity plates are in the floor and stairs, not in the bottom of the cavern," Deck said. He had a strangely excited tone, despite the situation.

"But how strong is the artificial gravity, though?" Merton asked. "If it twists all the way upside down, we still might fall."

"Don't you get it?" Vichna asked, hopping slightly on her stair. From the perspective of the others, it probably looked like she was defying physics by going up and down at an angle. "We're in deep space. There is no such thing as upside down or right-side up. If the gravity failed, you probably wouldn't even fall. You'd float."

Merton looked out over the abyss beneath them, or above them, or next to them, according to Vichna's point of view. "If the gravity only works over floors, then what's to prevent us from just finding an open path between here and the sphere, and just floating across?"

It was a good question. Vichna rustled through her supply bag and found an empty container from the emergency rations they had eaten earlier. With a windup, she threw the container out in the direction of the central sphere, a good solid pitch that would have sent it a considerable distance even in normal gravity. Instead of going straight like it would have in zero-g or eventually arcing downward like in standard gravity, the container veered in a curious corkscrew zigzag pattern as all the artificial gravity fields around it each vied for control of its path. Very quickly, it was no longer heading for the center of the chamber. It spun off to the side, far away from anywhere they wanted to go. It was difficult for Vichna to tell the farther away it got, but it appeared to be accelerating. Finally, just before it got far enough away that none of them could track it anymore, one of the gravity fields got a firm hold of it, and it smashed into, according to Vichna's perspective, an upside-down walkway. The sound of it hitting was loud enough that they could hear it echoing across the distance, letting her know with a high degree of certainty that, had it been one of them, they would be dead.

"Okay, then. Let's not do that," Deck said.

"So our only path is through this maze," Merton said. "How do we know there's a way for us to get through at all?"

"We don't," Vichna said. "It's probably just as much of a trap as anything else. But there has to be some way through. Harvey would have needed a path in the event that she for some reason couldn't use the main walkway."

"That only leaves one question, then," Lussa said. "The right stairs down or the left stairs up?"

Vichna resisted the urge to again clarify that up and down were relative in here. "Maybe we shouldn't all take the same path."

"I thought you were supposed to be the smart one," Deck said. "Splitting up is never, ever a good idea."

"It might be if one path ends up very clearly being the wrong one," Vichna said.

"So if two of us go down the right path and two go down the wrong one, the only two of us die instead of all four," Merton said. "Professor, I wouldn't exactly call that a comforting thought."

Vichna looked once more at the confusing maze of stairs and paths that filled the cavern. It didn't look like there was anything particularly deadly about the maze, but she had to consider the idea that there was something particularly nasty waiting for them somewhere among its impossible twists and turns. "We'll take a vote. Two groups of two or all of us together? You already know what I think."

Deck stared thoughtfully at his feet for several seconds before answering. "We can communicate with the other group through our helmets. Seeing this mess through two different perspectives might give us a better insight on how to get through it."

Merton turned to Lussa. "You get to either decide this or lock up the vote."

Lussa didn't hesitate at all. "If Vichna thinks splitting up is the best course of action, then I trust her."

Merton sighed. "Fine. I'm outvoted. So who's going down which path?"

After some brief discussion, they decided it would be best if one of each of the heavily armed security personnel went with each group. Lussa and Deck walked across the platform to the other set of stairs while Merton joined Vichna. Vichna would have much preferred Lussa's company to Merton's, especially considering they were separating under the assumption that at least one of the teams would run into serious trouble. Vichna didn't want to watch helplessly as Lussa was brutally murdered on the far side of the chamber. At the same time, though, she suspected it might be easier to think clearly without Lussa by her side.

"Are you ready for this?" Vichna asked Merton.

"This is probably the part where I'm supposed to say that I was born ready, or some kind of nonsense like that. Is that what you want to hear?"

"I'd rather hear the truth."

"Really? Then here it is. I'm scared shitless. I have been since we set foot on the station, and I'm not seeing anything that would get me to change my mind now."

"Fair enough," Vichna said. She looked over her shoulder and nodded at Lussa and Deck that they were ready. At the same time, they all started up the stairs. Or down the stairs. Either term worked.

The stairs, at least at first, were wide enough that Merton and Vichna could go down them side by side. They continued to twist at all angles, causing Vichna to quickly lose all sense of orientation. The whole thing gave her a feeling of vertigo, and she found herself unbalanced every time she let go of the railing. Merton, despite the assistance of his exoskeleton, seemed to be experiencing the same thing.

"How are you two doing?" Vichna sent to the other team.

"Dizzy," Lussa said. "Can you see us?"

Vichna looked back in the direction of the platform, which from her perspective now looked like it was on its side. "Where are you?"

"Not back that way. Look in front of you. Your eleven o'clock."

She looked in that direction, but at first didn't see anything. Then she realized they wouldn't necessarily be right in front of her and instead looked up. Lussa and Deck were on a platform above and to Vichna's left. They were already quite some distance away, but that wasn't the most distracting thing. From Vichna's perspective, they were hanging completely upside down, dangling in the air with nothing preventing them from falling.

"Okay, that's… that's… that's actually kind of fun," Vichna said. "I know I shouldn't be saying that given the circumstances, but still…"

"I'm right there with you," Lussa said. "But we're definitely going to get lost quickly this way."

"Wait, we don't have to," Deck said. "I've got an idea. First, let's beam the signal from each of our helmet cams to each other."

It took them nearly a minute to synchronize their suits together and then rearrange the individual video feeds on Vichna's display so it didn't interfere with her vision of whatever was directly in front of her. They had to stay switched from mid-gamma back to normal communications, or else everyone talking would take up too much room on the screen, but they all agreed that, for the moment at least, there wasn't much they could do to keep their communications from Harvey's avatar and the Void anyway. Having to stop to read everything everyone said would only be a distraction. Once that was all set, Deck had them each bring up the projection map they'd been building of the inside of the Void as they'd passed through it. The fairly straight-forward path of early had turned into a confusing jumble, but with them in two separate groups, they were gathering twice as much data about their route. With very little effort, they were all able to see their exact distance from each other, as well as their orientation compared to everything else. It was a lot of information to take in at once, but Vichna agreed that it could be the extra bit of help that might get them through this.

For several more minutes, both groups continued on their paths with no incident, although without their suits creating the map as they went, Vichna had to admit they would already be helplessly lost. Both paths had forked and forked again, increasing the chances that either group would make the wrong choice, but they collectively decided it was best not to break down their groups to less than two people, purely for safety's sake. Vichna led the way down (up?) another set of stairs and then stopped, a sigh caught in her throat. The stairs led to a platform, and then nothing else. It looked like they had found their way into a dead end.

"Guess we're going to have to go back and find another way," Vichna said.

"Actually, I'm not sure about that. Take a look." He pointed up. Roughly five meters above them there was another platform. It looked identical to the one they were currently on except for the fact that it was upside down. A walkway came out its other end and corkscrewed for a while before becoming more stairs.

"I'm not sure how that's supposed to help us," Vichna said.

"You're the one who was just talking about how we have to stop thinking of gravity in absolute terms. Think about it."

Vichna walked to the center of the platform and looked straight up at the other. She thought she might know what Merton was getting at. Curious, she reached up as high as she could to the inverted platform. It was much too far away for her to touch, being just over twice her height away. But as she reached, she thought she felt a gentle tingle.

"Wait," Vichna said. "Maybe if I…" She jumped lightly, still keeping her hand extended, then abruptly pulled it back as a much more uncomfortable sensation went through her bones.

"Ugh. Damn," she said, holding the hand in front of her and checking to see if there was anything wrong with it. It was intact and the unpleasant sensation was gone, but it had felt like some invisible person had reached out and yanked at her.

No, she realized. Not an invisible person. An invisible force.

"What is it?" Merton asked. "Are you okay?"

"I'm fine. I felt the gravity from the other platform. For just a second, I was being pulled in two different directions." The force of it hadn't hurt, but it was hardly a feeling she had enjoyed. It wasn't every day that she could say she felt the pull of two completely different gravitational fields at the same time.

"So you think that's the way we've got to go?" Merton asked.

Vichna shrugged. It was a completely different way of thinking about their path through the maze, but she had already said they would need to do exactly that. "It's worth a try. I'll need a bit of help, I think."

He laced his fingers together and put his hands down to form a step. Bracing herself on his shoulders, she lifted herself up until her head began to feel the pull of the other gravity field. "Wow, that feels weird. Like my body is right side up but my head is hanging upside down."

"Try to twist once you're all the way through the barrier," Merton said. "Otherwise, you'll land right on your head."

It was the most awkward and disorienting thing she had ever tried, but eventually she got the majority of her body into the other gravitational field. The gravity did the rest of the work for her and she fell up. Or down. She painfully hit the floor on her shoulder, but Merton was right. It was better than taking a direct hit to the head.

When she looked up, Merton was standing on the ceiling. Or was she on the ceiling?

"Okay, I have to admit this is actually pretty neat," she said.

"Under other circumstances, I might agree," Merton said. "But I think I'll wait until we're back on the *Contra Besta* before I try to appreciate any of it."

His exoskeleton gave him a slight boost when jumping, so he got higher than she had. Vichna still needed to reach and grab his hand to pull him all the way into the next gravity field, though. For a brief, bewildering moment, they both hung in the air as the two fields competed for their mass. Then Merton managed to get the majority of his body through and he toppled to the floor.

"Deck, Lussa, did you see all that?" Vichna asked. "You might have to deal with something similar."

"Yes, we saw it," Lussa said. "And take a look at our video feeds."

Vichna made the feeds from Deck and Lussa's suits larger on her screen, showing that they had indeed come in contact with their own unique gravity puzzle. Instead of an interchangeable floor and ceiling, though, their path had come to an abrupt halt. Where it stopped, though, there was a wall on their left side that continued on over the abyss. Vichna already knew what that meant before they started to experiment with the wall. Lussa reached out to touch the wall and expressed the same dismay Vichna had at the sudden shift in gravity. It took some peculiar acrobatics, but after a couple of minutes, both Lussa and Deck had crawled onto the wall, which was now their floor. Looking back, their former path was now a wall with nothing beneath it.

"This entire place is giving me a headache," Deck said.

"I'm right there with you," Merton said.

"Still, if that's the worst this maze has for us," Lussa stated, "then we should consider ourselves lucky."

Deck visibly recoiled from Lussa like she had a highly contagious virus. "Oh Lussa, please tell me you didn't just say that."

That, of course, was when the screeching began.

14

At first, the horrid noise didn't have a discernible source. It echoed all around them, coming from everywhere and nowhere in the cavern, and the echo effect was only enhanced since Vichna also heard it through the comms of the other three crew members.

"I'm pretty sure that's our cue to stop taking this leisurely," Merton said.

The high-pitched noise became more focused, and Vichna realized it wasn't coming from one single source but rather at least four. After a few more seconds, the noise sorted itself out in her mind into something she vaguely recognized. They were engines of some sort, although she couldn't be sure exactly what kind. Small, though, the kind that might be used for automated sentry drones.

Deck must have come to that conclusion at the same time. "Lussa, run!"

At that, all four of them ran down their walkways. Vichna ran up a set of stairs that abruptly twisted to the side so they were protruding from the side of where they had started. Halfway up (although they had switched orientation with the twist so that they somehow felt like they were going down), she stopped just long enough to look in the direction of the nearest sound. She saw a flat, white object that looked vaguely like an Old-Earth manta ray, except there was a stalk protruding from one side that appeared to be a weapon. She would have said the stalk was on top, but the drone itself didn't make any attempt to differentiate between up and down. It was flying across the empty spaces and heading right for Vichna and Merton. She had no doubt that it wasn't alone.

"Don't let any of them get too close!" she yelled. From some distance, she thought she heard the thrum of a laser hitting something, and Vichna risked looking at Lussa's feed long enough to see that a beam had hit just in front of them to scorch the walkway. Rather than trying to run, Lussa stopped and aimed her weapon. The drone looked like it was preparing another shot when Lussa fired. Her beam clipped the drone's wing, sending it spinning away out of sight, although Vichna didn't think it looked like it was completely out of commission.

"I'm only detecting four of them," Merton said. "We should stop and take them out!"

"Negative!" Lussa said. "I'm picking up at least six more coming at us from the direction of the central sphere."

"And I think I see two more coming from below where we came in." Strictly speaking, she thought they might be coming from hatches on either side of the door, but this was hardly the time to debate direction.

"I think this is quickly becoming more than we can fight," Deck said. Merton aimed and fired at the drone that had been approaching them. He missed, and the drone returned fire. There was a flash of sparks against Merton's arm and he screamed. Vichna thought she saw a little spray of blood, but the exoskeleton had taken the worst of the hit. Whatever kind of laser these things were using, they weren't as destructive as what they'd found in the turret room, but they were still dangerous. Vichna pulled out her pistol and fired blindly at the drone. She was shocked that she actually scored a hit, causing the drone to veer away and out of sight.

"Merton's hit!" Vichna said. "I don't think we're going to be able to stay and fight these things."

"My map says we're about halfway to the central sphere," Lussa said. "At the very least, if we get a solid structure at our back, we won't have to worry about anything coming at us from behind."

"Go then!" Vichna said. "Everyone try to get to the sphere!" She turned to Merton. "Can you still run?"

"Uh, it hit my arm, not my legs."

"Right," Vichna said, flushing. "Let's go."

They ran as fast as they could, although Merton had to actually slow himself to stay by Vichna's side thanks to the exoskeleton's more powerful stride. She heard more whining from the drones, including a few shots from Lussa and Deck's position as they had to stop briefly to chase off the drones before they could get through another particularly tricky gravity trap. Vichna and

Merton ran into another of their own in short order, and they both had to skid to a halt to avoid flying over a sudden edge in their walkway. As Merton turned around to lay down cover fire, Vichna did her best to concentrate and figure out what they were supposed to do here.

Looking over the edge, there was nothing for nearly a hundred meters, while about ten meters across the gap the walkway started again. Looking up, she saw what might as well have been the missing part of the walkway, except it was twenty meters up and upside down. There didn't appear to be any easy way to reach it, and even if they could simply jump into its gravity field like the one earlier, the fall up would have been far enough to cause them both some serious hurt.

A laser flew past Vichna's head. "Whatever we've got to do, you better figure it out quick," Merton said. "Three of them coming up from behind and above, er, below, er, something."

Vichna looked up at the inverted piece of walkway dangling in the air, apparently held there by its own gravity and anti-gravity fields. The fields on the previous walkways and stairs had extended up about three meters or so, but she realized that didn't mean all the walkways had the same amount of pull. Just to check, Vichna jumped up and waved her hand out over the gap. Sure enough, she felt like something was trying to pull her arms up.

"We need to jump across the gap," she said. Merton rapidly fired several shots, taking out one of the drones and causing the other two to spread out.

"Are you crazy?" Merton asked. "Even with a boost from my exoskeleton, that's too far. We'll fall."

"We might," Vichna agreed, "just not in the direction you think." Before he could ask her any questions, Vichna backed up from the edge about a meter, prepped herself, and then took a running leap off the edge.

A few more lasers passed over her, one getting dangerously close to her head and causing the faceplate to darken in an effort to protect her eyes from the flash. It couldn't have happened at a worse time, but Vichna hoped she wouldn't need her full eyesight to do this. Just as she left the walkway, she felt gravity reverse, pulling her up to the inverted walkway above. Her forward moment continued, though, and to anyone watching, the result it probably looked like she was defying physics by going up but not coming down. The extra boost carried her across the gap, although when the gravity went back to where she had started, she was a good two and a half meters still up in the air. She crashed and rolled on the walkway, almost dropping her pistol, but she got a hold of it just before it slid over the side. Vichna got to her knees and turned around, aiming the pistol to give Merton cover fire.

"Do it!" she yelled at him. He looked surprised at her feat, but he didn't pause to make any kind of exclamation of wonder. He took a running jump as well. One of the drones came up behind him, looking dangerously close, and Vichna shot it out of the air.

Damn, she thought. *When did I get so good with one of these things?* As if to spite that thought, the next couple of shots went wide, but the drones had broken off and buzzed away, undoubtedly preparing to come at them from another direction.

Vichna took just enough time to make sure that Lussa and Deck were still moving, then she stood up and ran so fast that her lungs burned. Her survival suit did its best to give her the extra oxygen she needed, but as advanced as it might be, there was only so much it could do.

"We're almost there!" Merton said. Another beam shot from somewhere they couldn't see, this time clipping his exoskeleton in the calf. Although it didn't look like the beam had gone through the tough shell, there was no doubting the exoskeleton was damaged when Merton's speed abruptly slowed. Vichna turned in the direction the beam had come from to squeeze off a shot. Despite barely aiming, her shot hit the drone right in its stalk. It continued flying, but the directionless way it moved seemed to imply it was more or less dead.

"Look," Vichna said. "Up or down or sideways on those stairs. I think that's what we're looking for."

Up ahead, another of the impossible staircases twisted on its side before going onto a long, corkscrew-shaped path. At the end of the path, Vichna could finally see a large platform right against the enormous central sphere. And right where the sphere and platform met was one of those red spots. If there had been any doubt at a distance, Vichna could now say for certain that the red thing was a door.

"Go, go, go!" Merton said. "I'll cover you."

Something about the sound of his voice made Vichna believe he expected this to be his last stand. "Oh no you don't. We're both going to get there together."

The exoskeleton was leaking some kind of fluid from the leg, and with every movement, Merton slowed more. He eventually had to abandon his heavy rifle, as the suit no longer had the power to hold it up. Vichna stayed by his side, firing wildly behind them and marveling every time it sounded like she had actually hit something. She didn't turn back to look, though. There weren't that many more engine sounds directly behind them, but she did think there might be a few directly ahead.

"Vichna, down here!" Lussa said. Vichna risked taking a moment to look over the edge, then remembered that down had many different meanings here. Checking Lussa's feed and seeing herself, Vichna figured to look up and to her right, where Lussa and Deck were racing along a walkway of their own, hanging upside down and at an angle to her. Vichna followed the path of their walkway and saw that it, too, led into the corkscrew. While Vichna and Merton had managed to shake off most of the drones, Lussa and Deck still had four of them coming up close behind. Vichna took a couple of potshots at them, clipping one.

"Get to that corkscrew thing," Vichna said. "It looks more defensible than anything else out here."

"You don't need to tell me twice," Lussa said. Vichna turned all her concentration back to getting to the corkscrew herself, and within a minute, they had arrived at the corkscrew's beginning.

While Lussa and Deck came down a set of stairs toward them, stairs that were now finally oriented the same as Vichna was herself, Vichna stared at the corkscrew and tried to figure out what it was even supposed to be. Roughly cylindrical, the path inside it went up about twenty-five meters and curved around, the curve tight enough that only about a meter separated the path as it curved back around next to itself. This went down for, according to her suit's censors, nearly a hundred meters before it came out on the platform. It was their last visible obstacle before what they believed was the vault. As such, Vichna was unnerved. It looked way too easy.

"Come on, let's go," Deck said as they caught up with Vichna and Merton. Merton took Vichna's pistol and used it against the drones that were now buzzing back and forth behind them. Although the drones were still taking shots, they seemed reluctant to get too close to the corkscrew. There was no way that could be a good sign.

"Wait. Maybe we should examine this thing a little closer first," Vichna said. Lussa had taken up a position next to Merton. She shot down two more drones. They fell out of the air easily, getting caught up in the weird currents of gravity and flying apparent in unpredictable directions.

"We don't have the time," Merton said. "Your pistol is running low on charge, and these things aren't going to let us go back to find a different route. Just go through!"

"This is most definitely a trap," Vichna said.

One of the drones shot Lussa.

Vichna screamed and ran for her, but Lussa held up a hand to indicate she should stay back. Her exoskeleton was still in better shape than Merton's, who had to start shedding pieces of it in order to move, but she looked like she was in pain.

"We've got to go through," Lussa said. "No other choice."

Vichna nodded. "Okay. Then I'm going first."

Lussa sounded like she wanted to protest, but her words came out as nothing more than a pained groan. She clutched her ribs, making Vichna wonder if the shot had done something to her insides. There wasn't any time to speculate, unfortunately.

Without giving herself any more time to think, Vichna turned and ran into the corkscrew. The rest followed, Merton, then Deck, then Lussa. When Vichna took her first step onto the swirling platform, she was immediately disoriented as she felt a large number of gravity fields pulling on her at once. This was like the transition between the upside down and right-side up platforms earlier, but constant and from many more directions. The fields on this pathway were strong enough, she realized, that she didn't just feel the one below her feet but also the ones to her side and above.

The gap between the part of the path she was on and the part where it twirled around next to her again was small, but given she could barely make herself stand in this gravitational soup, she highly doubted her ability to leap between them and cut the journey through the corkscrew short. The only logical way through was to run straight down the path, which to the orientation of anyone on the outside would look like she was running up the wall and then on the ceiling before coming back around.

She almost hesitated, her mind trying to rebel at what it insisted was physically impossible, but more shots from the drones spurred her into movement. Vichna ran at her top speed, although for several seconds, she had the oddest sensation that she wasn't going anywhere at all. From her perspective, she might as well have been inside a giant hamster wheel, the structure moving beneath her while she stayed in place. Yet when she looked back outside the corkscrew, it looked like all of existence beyond was rotating around her, the drones and the platform and the entire confusing maze beyond spinning with her at the center.

Vichna tripped, almost falling through the gap at her side, then stood back up and resolved to look at the outside world as little as possible. As long as she kept her eyes forward on the path, she wouldn't get dizzy or disoriented. Curses from behind her told her that the others were experiencing the same thing, but she didn't dare look back to check on them. That would only trip her up again and there was no telling where she might go flying if she went through the gap.

There was one thing she couldn't help but notice, though, something that was both calming and alarming at the same time: the drones had stopped shooting and following. It was calming because she suddenly felt like she was safe, that she could tackle this last challenge with no need to worry about outside forces. It was alarming because she knew it couldn't be that easy. If the drones weren't after them anymore, it had to be for a reason, and she couldn't imagine a reason that was good for her or the rest of the crew.

From the outside, the corkscrew hadn't looked that long, and she'd thought they'd be able to get through it quickly. The entire structure, after all, was far shorter than the rest of the maze they had just run. Appearances were deceiving, she now realized, as the corkscrew didn't allow them to go straight through. Going around the inside of the corkscrew made for a much longer journey than it had looked. Even though she was in great shape and the suit was assisting her breathing as much as possible, Vichna felt herself tiring from the exertion. All her limbs felt like they were getting heavier as she…

Wait.

That wasn't just exhaustion. There was a deep vibration under her feet as some kind of machinery within the corkscrew began to work harder, getting slowly and steadily deeper. And with every second that passed, it became just a little bit harder to move. At the same time, she thought she could feel an increased pull above and all around.

The gravity inside the corkscrew was increasing.

"We've got to get out of this thing now!" Merton screamed. Even though he was wounded, he ran harder and pulled up even with Vichna. "We're not going to make it this way. We need to jump across the gaps!"

Vichna would have protested, but Merton never gave her the chance. He cut in front of her and tried to leap across to the next section of the path. His jump probably would have been graceless under the best of circumstances, but with the gravity slowly and steadily increasing, he only barely made it across, his heels hanging over the abyss for a moment. Before she could debate the intelligence of this, she did the same. Without any injury, she managed to do slightly better, but not by much. Instead of not making it, she hit the path hard and slid forward. In this instance, the greater gravity probably saved her, as she probably would have slid right off otherwise. Behind her, she heard both Deck and Lussa jumping, although they were above and left of her relatively. They didn't sound like they were handling the increased gravity any better, and she could only feel it getting stronger.

That's why the drones didn't follow us, Vichna thought. *And why they barely harmed us in the first place. We were being herded into here*. And if they stayed, she had no doubt that the gravity would continue growing until it crushed their fragile bodies.

"Don't jump the gaps!" Vichna screamed behind (above? Below? In front of?) her. "Just keep running!" As she struggled to her feet, Deck caught up with her, giving her a hand up that barely seemed to make a difference. The gravity was starting to feel painful, a force pushing down on her and grinding her bones against each other.

Merton was the first one out the other side. While the path came to a stop right against the platform, Merton jumped free earlier. From the platform, it would have looked like he was jumping off the wall, and he had to twist in the air at the sudden shift in gravity. As the gravity was also lighter over the platform, the extra push he'd given himself to get out of the corkscrew sent him flying farther than he'd probably intended. He hit the platform faceplate first and then stopped moving.

Vichna came out next, with Deck right behind her. The instant she was out of the corkscrew's gravity field, she felt lighter, a sudden change that again caused her to stumble. She looked to Merton, realizing he might be dead or unconscious, but before she could do anything for him, she heard the corkscrew's deep base hum get louder.

And, she realized, only three of them had come out of it.

She turned to see Lussa on, according to Vichna's current perspective, the ceiling of the corkscrew. She had collapsed to her knees and was trying to shed what she still wore of the exoskeleton. Not only was it weighing her down, but her breathing was harsh and ragged. The thrum deepened, and Lussa visibly fought against the gravity, as though it was a physically sitting on her shoulders and crushing her.

"Lussa!" Vichna screamed, but before she could try anything, Deck was already rushing back in, stooping under the pressure again as soon as he set foot on the corkscrew. Lussa wasn't that far in, but unless she got all her extra equipment off, she might not have the strength to get that short distance to safety. Whatever mechanism generated the gravity in the corkscrew was now working so hard that it shook the platform they were all standing on. By the time Deck got to the top of the loop, he himself could barely stand, but that didn't stop him from helping Lussa shed the exoskeleton. After a few more pieces were off, she struggled to her feet, but even that didn't last long. She fell back down.

The deep hum grew in pitch.

"No! Lussa, no!" Vichna screamed. She wanted to run back in, but she knew there was nothing she would be able to do in time. Lussa looked at her.

"I love you," Lussa said through their comms.

"Uh-uh. None of that," Deck said. "I saw too many tearful good-byes during the war. No more." Gathering his every last bit of strength, Deck shoved her out to the end of the corkscrew.

For several horrible seconds, it didn't look like his effort wasn't going to be enough. Even as Lussa approached the edge, she looked like the gravity was going to keep its hold on her. Then her shoulder left the gravity field, then her arm, her head. Deck kept pushing, forcing her out over the invisible barrier between the two fields. Her chest came out, then her hips. That seemed to be enough for the main platform's gravity to get a firm hold of her, causing her to drop toward the platform. At the last second, Lussa tried to reach back in and grab Deck's hand. They clasped, Lussa's weight and momentum pulling Deck to more of a standing position.

They both held on tight for a few more seconds. Vichna saw what was about to happen, but didn't have the time to voice her fear. The bizarre gravitational antics would cause Lussa to swing on Deck's arm, and the momentum would bring her right back into the corkscrew.

Deck must have understood that too, because he let go.

Lussa slammed into the platform, but unlike Merton, who was still prone, she immediately stood back up and turned to rescue Deck. Vichna grabbed her, though, holding her back from getting any closer to the corkscrew again. Lussa tried to fight it for a moment. Then she stopped, understanding just as much as Deck and Vichna did that this was over.

Lussa's weight and pull had nearly dislodged Deck from the gravity field, but it hadn't been enough. Instead, it pulled him down into the center of the corkscrew and held him there, the competing gravitational forces all trying to claim him. Deck's voice abruptly cut off, but he was still moving. He'd cut his own comm channel, Vichna realized. He didn't want anyone else to hear him screaming.

Hanging in the air, the walls of the corkscrew pulled at Deck's limbs until he was splayed out in a grotesque impression of some old drawing Vichna had once seen from old Earth. One of the pieces of art Captain Harvey was supposed to have here, actually, not that Vichna cared much about any of that anymore. The walls all pulled at him equally. Even as the gravity generator got louder, Vichna still thought she could hear the sound of Deck's bones snapping.

Where Lussa had been seconds earlier, the discarded pieces of her exoskeleton appeared to melt as gravity crushed them. Vichna had no idea how much force would be required to actually do such a thing, but she knew it wasn't supposed to be easy. Conversely, while the pieces of armor flattened, Deck himself seemed to grow. His limbs and neck elongated, slowly at first then with increasing rapidity. The tips of his suit's gloves burst, tiny pieces of the material flying to the walls. The bottom of his boots burst open, and soon after so did the flesh of his feet. Blood poured out and painted the corkscrew, not making even the slightest splash as it hit.

Several of his fingers ripped off. Then more parts of his suit. Scraps of flesh, pieces of bone. The helmet ripped off and was instantly crushed against the floor. It took part of Deck's jaw with it, and now that there was nothing between them, Vichna could clearly hear his inhuman warbles of pain.

Something vital gave out inside Deck's body, and he exploded. Pieces of him splattered against the inside of the corkscrew and were instantly crushed.

As if aware that its job was done, the hum of the extra gravity slowed down and eventually came to a stop.

15

There were no tears this time, no throwing up. Vichna and Lussa were just numb, their brains no longer even accepting the horrors they had witnessed. They checked on Merton and found him slowly coming to. He'd taken a hard thump when he'd hit the ground, but his helmet had taken the brunt of the damage. He had to remove it in order to see, though, as the faceplate was completely smashed. Lussa, too, had to remove her helmet, as some vital piece of technology inside must have been damaged by the gravity generator, resulting in the interior screen showing her nothing but black. They would have all been concerned about whether Merton or Lussa could survive some kind of environmental attack, but Vichna could see without even asking them that neither of them believed any more that there was any real chance of any of them getting out of the Void alive.

Merton took one look back at the corkscrew and immediately knew without anyone having to tell him what had become of Deck. He looked away quickly and got a faraway look in his eyes. Vichna wondered if he was remembering his moment in bed with Deck and Gregs, or if there was some other fond memory coming to him that he simply wanted to keep to himself. Lussa got as close as she dared to the corkscrew again, then dropped to her knees again and performed another Mutaban prayer. It was different than the last one, with different hand gestures likely meant to reflect the circumstances of Deck's death, but Vichna didn't ask her for details this time. Lussa had a haunted sound to her voice that made Vichna wonder if the girl blamed herself for what had happened to Deck, but now wasn't the time to ask.

While she let them have their moment to mourn Deck, Vichna took a quick survey of what resources they still had. Not that they'd had much to start with, but now they were down to next to nothing. Both Lussa and Merton had been forced to abandon their weapons, which was just as well considering neither of them had enough left of their exoskeletons to actually carry the massive things. Merton had still been holding her pistol when he dove out of the corkscrew, but when she retrieved it from him she saw that the charge was so low it would only be good for three or four more carefully placed shots at the most. Vichna was also the only one who still had a functioning helmet for her survival suit, which meant not only that she was the only one protected from environmental hazards, but that she was also the only one with enhanced sensors, map data, video recording, and even light. Both Lussa and Merton were injured. Lussa looked like she would be able to continue on, even if it was in pain, but Merton was bleeding in several places and only barely looked capable of walking. Vichna would have done her best to patch him up, except she discovered that at some point during the chase she had lost her supply bag. As best as she could tell, it had likely fallen through one of the gaps in the corkscrew. She supposed she could play back her video recordings to be sure, although that wouldn't do much good. The bag would be no less lost, and there was no way she was getting it back.

The only positive thing she could see was that the drones had vanished. She'd lost track of them while everyone had been trying to get out of the corkscrew. She understood why they wouldn't follow the group into the trap, but now that they were out the other side, tired and injured, she didn't understand why the drones didn't just fly around and pick them off.

No, she realized, she did actually understand. That would have been too easy. Harvey's avatar wouldn't find it entertaining enough. Which only made her wonder what still might be waiting for them ahead.

That thought caught in her head, and she finally turned around to face the sphere and recognize what it meant. Unless they were very wrong in their predictions, this was it. The reason the Void existed in the first place. Captain Melissa Harvey's fabled vault.

They had known from a distance that the structure was huge, but it was a completely different thing to witness up close. The sphere alone was several times bigger than the *Contra Besta*. The platform they currently stood on was one of many, each one connected to the rest of the gravity maze with some other contraption that was no doubt just as deadly as the corkscrew. At every platform there was a red, round door. Unlike the rest of the station, there were lights here, so Vichna hoped there was enough power that they wouldn't need to open their door with another manual-release lever.

And next to the door, of course, was a hard-light generator. Vichna didn't approach it yet. She waited patiently until Lussa and Merton were done and came to her.

"So is this it?" Lussa asked. "Is this the whole reason this place is here?"

Vichna tried to respond, but her body was wracked by a momentary spasm of pain. It went away quickly, but various indicators on her screen told her that there were anomalies throughout her body. She shut those indicator functions off. Vichna already knew perfectly well what that meant. The mid-gamma transmissions had begun affecting her genetic integrity. If Lussa and Merton weren't feeling the same thing right now, that was only because the pain was covered up by their various injuries. The problems would only get worse from here on out. While she turned off her suit's ability to monitor her vitals, she kept a small countdown clock running in the upper corner of her vision. They had roughly seven or six hours before they reached the point of no return.

"Are you okay?" Lussa asked.

"I'll be fine. And yes, I think this is it."

"I don't know," Merton said. "It doesn't look like there's any way out from here."

Vichna had to admit it looked that way, but she still thought there was a chance. From their current orientation, the sphere hung from a long pillar that dropped down from the ceiling high above. Bringing up her rough map, she saw that there were several of the possible escape pods not far from the place where the pillar and roof met. If there was some way up from inside, then there might still be a chance that they could live.

"We'll see," Vichna said. "Are you two ready for this?"

"I don't think such a thing is possible," Merton muttered.

Lussa, however, had a more determined look. "Yes. We're ready."

Vichna stopped for a long moment to gaze into Lussa's eyes.

In this moment, she didn't see a child. Merton and his people were right. No matter what the rest of society said, Lussa was a full-grown woman, capable of everything else an adult could do. That included persevering even when there didn't appear any logical reason to keep going.

Vichna realized with a shock that she might just be in love with her. And from the way Lussa stared back at her, not to mention her words earlier, the feeling was mutual.

"We're going to get out of here," Vichna said.

"Yes, we absolutely are," Lussa agreed.

"Not if I bleed to death first," Merton grumbled. "Can we please get moving?"

They had to hold Merton up as they walked across the platform to the door. Vichna couldn't help but notice he left a small trail of blood drops behind them. She wasn't a doctor, but she knew that Merton probably had less time than either she or Lussa did. Although the clock continued to count down, Vichna mentally removed about four or five hours. That was how much time he had, at best. The equipment back on the *Contra Besta* would be able to take care of those wounds right along with the mid-gamma degradation, but he had to get there first.

The hard-light generator whirred to life as soon as they began approaching, and by the time they reached the door, Harvey's hologram was waiting for them, her hands on her hips and an annoyed expression on her face as though they had taken far too long to get this far.

"Alright, confession time," Harvey said once they were finally in front of her. "The main bridge wasn't hard-light at all. You could have walked across it with no problem."

"Pretty sure you're lying," Lussa said.

"And why would you say that?" Harvey asked.

"Because you think it's funnier that way?" Merton guessed.

"Okay, sure, you've got me. Or maybe you don't. I guess you'll never know for sure whether you could have gone that way or not."

"Knock it off," Vichna said. "You had your fun and got another bloodbath. Is this where you throw something else at us?"

"Nope. I've got nothing more." A new expression came to

Harvey, one Vichna didn't think she'd even seen in old recordings
of the real woman. She looked flustered. "From this point on, I
don't have control of anything else. Everything beyond belongs to
the other one."

"What other one?" Vichna asked. "Who else is here?"

"Who else indeed? I guess you'll just have to go forward and
find out. I've got to warn you all, though. You are really not
going to be happy with what you find."

"If you don't think we'll like it, then I'm going to venture a
guess that we'll think it's just fine," Vichna said.

"Ha! Keep telling yourself that. Don't say I didn't warn you.
So go ahead. We'll meet up again at the end." She smiled, an oily
and disturbing expression that made Vichna's skin crawl. "One
last time."

Harvey disappeared. The group took a few more steps forward,
and the red door slid open for them.

They all paused, half-expecting one more trap to come at them
as they walked through, but when they finally got the nerve to go
through, nothing happened except for the door closing behind
them. Vichna tested it to see if they could go back, but the door
wouldn't open. Not that there was anything that way they wanted
to get back to.

The room beyond was completely dark, although from the
echo, they could tell it was another large chamber. Perhaps not as
large as the gravity maze, but definitely larger even than the first
room they'd come through. The light on Vichna's helmet broke
through some of the gloom, just enough for her to see that they
were on a balcony that continued on to their left and right, curving
slightly with the inside of the sphere. Looking up and down, she
could see other balconies, presumably for people coming in
through the other doors. Beyond that, the light didn't penetrate far
enough them to see much.

"Kind of disappointing," Merton said. "So much for your
unimaginable treasure, Professor."

"Wait," Vichna said. "The ambient light is increasing." She
turned off the lamp on her helmet and relied entirely on her
readout. Yes, tiny lights along the edge of the balcony were
slowly turning up, as if designed to keep them from being blinded

by a sudden outpouring of light. As the lights came up, she saw ladders and stairs coming off each balcony and leading down to someplace closer to the center of the room. From the pattern that the lights were turning on, they were very clearly intended to guide their way to whatever was next.

"Doesn't look like we have much choice but to follow them," Lussa said. They both got a firmer grip on Merton and helped him to the nearest set of stairs.

Right as they reached the first step, the lights in the entire chamber brightened considerably. They all had to look away for a moment until their eyes adjusted.

When they looked back to the center of the chamber, all three of them gasped at once.

Two hundred years ago, a mad woman had gone on a rampage across the galaxy. She'd stolen, pillaged, and plundered, all in the name of preserving what she considered to be pure. The things she had stolen had become nothing but a legend, a bed-time story.

But after pursuing it, Vichna had finally proven the stories true.

They were in the presence of the lost treasure of Captain Melissa Harvey, Pirate Queen of Deep Space.

16

There was so much to see that, at first, Vichna had trouble getting a comprehensive idea of what she was exactly seeing. In the center of the spherical chamber, going all the way from the bottom to the top, there was a thick cylinder consisting of round floors. At a rough guess, Vichna thought the cylinder might be about fifteen stories tall. It didn't have any walls, instead being held up by a large number of load-bearing pillars connecting each floor. The outer edge of each floor except the bottom was surrounded by a railing.

Each floor was covered in shelves. And on the shelves were the lost treasures of an entire galaxy.

"Wow," Lussa said. "That's a lot of stolen artifacts."

Vichna could only nod. Despite the pain and horror of the last several hours, she felt almost giddy. People had died. More might even die before this was over. Yet the goal she'd been working toward for most of her life had been achieved. She'd found the Void. She'd found its treasure.

So now what the hell was she supposed to do with herself?

That was a question to answer at some later time. For now, they simply needed to find a way out. They didn't even have time to do a comprehensive search of the collection. Time was still ticking. If they made it out of here alive, someone would eventually come back, and this time with a better idea of what to expect, along with the tools and talent to counteract the Void's deadly traps. Vichna didn't even care if she wasn't one of the ones who came to claim it. She'd found it, and that was enough. Once they were on the *Contra Besta* again, *if* they made it back to the *Contra Besta*, Vichna never wanted to see this place again.

Still, as they hobbled their way down the stairs, Vichna couldn't help but be curious. "We probably have to go through the collection to get out," she said. "Unless there's some other way through the maze…"

"I am definitely not going back through the maze," Merton

said.

"...then the only possible way through is up." She looked up at the top story of the collection, or at least the top story she could see from here. It looked to her like the collection might continue up the inside of the outer pillar, but they wouldn't be sure until they made it that far.

They stopped at the bottom of the stairs, gazing reverently at the collection in front of them. Even Merton, who by all means should have been egging them on to move faster, let his jaw drop at the sight. The entered the warren of shelves on the first story, not able to help themselves as they stopped and occasionally looked at the assembled oddities.

If Harvey had intended this place to be her own personal museum, she sure hadn't organized it like one. In fact, just at first glance, Vichna didn't think there was any organization to it at all. The shelves ranged from plastic bookcases to large, industrial steel shelves, with the steel sometimes used to hold tiny objects and plastic used for heavy ones, so much so that several of the plastic shelves had bowed under two hundred years of pressure. Vichna stopped to look at one such item, a lump of jagged metallic substance. She thought she might have seen similar things in other museums, a lump of inner-core meteor that by itself was probably enough to pay for this entire station. There were also some jewels, most of them unlabeled, but a few with small etched plaques next to them denoting where they had come from. She stopped at one and stared at it in awe as her memory of history recalled the name next to it: the Hope Diamond.

"Stairs," Merton said. He sounded weak. As much as Vichna wanted to explore, he was a constant reminder that they didn't have the time. He pointed to a stairwell in the center of the displays, and Vichna and Lussa wasted no time in dragging Merton there and helping him up. The stairs spiraled upward through all the floors, allowing them to keep going without stop, although Vichna couldn't help but look at all the things they passed on the way up.

Here was a piece of peculiar engine that she thought might have been from the *Converter*, the first ever interstellar space-fold-capable ship. There was a flickering digital screen with some king of blueprints on it, and although Vichna didn't recognize the structure it represented, she got the impression it was supposed to be big, larger even than the Central Diplomacy Building on New Genysis, which was at this time considered to be the single largest human-made structure in existence. They passed one floor that was dedicated entirely to art, and Vichna marveled at the original DeTernio prints, paintings from Huronin and Machtoy. Some looked even older. There was a piece of wall with what might have been some kind of graffiti on it that look like it had been stenciled. She even thought she got a quick glimpse of the drawing she had thought of earlier, the one with the man inside the circle, his arms and legs splayed out. Next to it was the bottom half of what had once been a portrait, possibly of a woman in elegant clothing, but the painting was cut off just above the chin, where at some point in the past part of it had been burned. She found herself idly wondering what the woman's expression might have once been.

Up and up they went, past treasures both beautiful and inexplicable. On one floor, they found nothing but carved blocks of stone, possibly the last pieces of structures created by long-dead civilizations. The next was rare, old pieces of technology. Vichna thought she recognized one of the earliest models of portable particle accelerators, which she knew would be worth a fortune on the private collectors' market. Another floor seemed be nothing but stacks of precious metals in all forms, from bars to rings to coins and even, most disconcertingly, chips of shiny gold and red that were embedded in the back of mummified human hands. Vichna had no time to reflect on that one, as it was clear by then that they were all close to the top of the chamber. The staircase stopped winding upward and instead stopped, continuing at a flight of stairs closer to the edge.

"Do you think that's significant?" Lussa asked.

"I've think I've stopped trying to guess anything about this place," Vichna said. "This could mean something important. Or it could mean Captain Harvey's designer just got bored and decided to change the stairs up a little."

Nonetheless, they all exercised a little more caution as they approached these particular stairs. They went up into the ceiling of the chamber, undoubtedly into the bottom of the pillar they had seen from outside. Both Vichna and Lussa paused and took a deep breath before continuing up them. Merton tried to do the same, but all it got him was a coughing fit complete with tiny flecks of red in his phlegm.

"Don't know what's wrong with me, but I don't think I've got a whole lot longer," Merton said.

Vichna had a few educated guesses, but she was a historian, not a doctor. He was right. Unless they found some kind of med bay above them, he probably wasn't going to make it to any theoretical escape pods.

"Just hold on a bit longer," Lussa said, trying to hold back her own pained grunts. "We might go up these stairs and find Harvey's personal collection of rare super-cures."

"Or we'll get crushed by a death trap," Merton said.

Lussa nodded. "Or that. If it's option number two, then at least we can hope it's quick."

Once they made it to the top of the stairs, though, they found neither. In fact, there didn't appear to be anything at all on this level. No, Vichna realized. That wasn't correct at all. There was a large, glowing white circle in the middle of the floor. And above it, there was a long shaft, also illuminated in white light with no apparent source.

"Elevator, maybe?" Lussa asked.

"That would be my guess," Vichna said. "Do we risk getting on?"

"It's either that or go back down and out through the maze," Merton said. "I'd rather risk possible death instead of certain death."

"I guess it's decided, then," Vichna said. They led Merton to the glowing circle. Vichna stopped long enough to look for some kind of controls, but the circle was completely featureless. None of them asked how to work it, though. Instead, they all stepped into the middle and waited. After a few seconds, there was a quiet, almost calming hum, then the platform lifted into the air. Vichna had no idea what was propelling them upward, and at this point she didn't much care. She was feeling ragged and worn out, her body no longer obeying her as precisely as she wanted.

Symptoms of the mid-gamma poisoning, she supposed. She might have longer than Merton, but that timer in the corner of her screen still counted down.

Vichna had to darken her visor at the sudden brightness of the shaft. Merton and Lussa didn't have that option, both of them having to blink and hold a hand over their eyes before their vision adjusted. As such, Vichna was the first to realize the walls of the shaft weren't completely smooth. The elevator slowed down, and Vichna left the other two in the center while she took a closer look at the walls.

From a distance, the walls had seemed like they just had their own unique texture, but once Vichna was closer, she realized that wasn't true. The walls were, in fact, glass tubes and vials. Thousands of them, all ranging in size from the size of a small room down to the length of Vichna's pinky. Lussa gently set Merton down and came to join Vichna.

"What are they?" Lussa asked.

"They're, um, I think this might be the second half of Harvey's collection."

They both stared, watching as the glassed-in specimens slowly went down out of their sight. Looking up and around the shaft, Vichna made a rough estimate that there must have been hundreds of thousands of vials and jars, each and every single one containing something biological. The smallest vials held what looked like nothing more than water, although each one was marked with a small yellow biohazard symbol. Others were huge and contained the skulls of species that had long ago passed out of existence, both from Earth and a multitude of other planets. In between were the jars with preserved, whole animals.

"Her biological library," Vichna said. "Pure genetic samples. Things that haven't been tampered with. Maybe..." Her words cut off and she forgot what she was about to say as they rose past a series of glass containers holding actual humans. Several looked like they could almost still be alive, given how perfectly preserved their bodies were. Others were little more than skeletons and mummies. Neither Lussa nor Vichna spoke, each staring in horror at the contents of some of the glass coffins. Harvey wouldn't have kept anything she didn't think was pure, so

Vichna had no doubt that some of the better-preserved specimens had come from Harvey's own followers. There were men and women of all ages, even children as young as five years old. They rose past one woman, completely naked, who was visibly pregnant. That one, at least, was definitely dead. At some point in the past, the glass on her coffin had been broken near her face, and shards had embedded in her cheeks and eyes.

Lussa turned away. "Why?" she whispered. "Why would Harvey do this?"

"DNA samples," Vichna said. "In the event that she couldn't return the universe to her vision of purity through genocide, then she would do it through growing her own super species, I suppose."

"But I thought that whole idea was anathema to her," Vichna said. "Wouldn't a genetically engineered person be the same to her as people who'd gone through GT?"

Vichna shrugged. "I guess she had different ideas of what was and wasn't pure enough. Who can tell what she was thinking."

The majority of the humans slid down out of view, helping Vichna control the gorge that had been growing in her stomach. They were now at a series of other glass tubes, small enough that Vichna could grab them with her hand. Curiosity getting the better of her, and Vichna did exactly that, touching one of the tubes and almost dropping it when it easily came out of its slot on the wall.

"That probably wasn't a good idea," Lussa said.

Vichna quickly tried to put it back, only for the tube's slot to slide down out of sight. With no other choice but to continue holding it, she took a closer look at its contents. It was filled with some viscous fluid, and floating inside...

"What is that?" Lussa asked. "I've never seen anything like it."

Vichna stared at the small animal floating dead but perfectly preserved in the tube. Again, biology and paleontology were far from her areas of expertise, but she thought there was enough random knowledge for her to identify the brown-furred mammal by its striped back and stubby tail. "A chipmunk, I think."

"Never heard of it."

"They're extinct. Or at least they're supposed to be. Native to

Old Earth. As far as I was aware, they vanished long before Harvey's time."

"So how did she get one?"

It was a good question, but Vichna didn't have an answer. It was also a question she could have asked about most of the specimens tucked into the cylindrical wall. At lot of these creatures didn't look like they should still exist in the universe. Beyond just the samples clearly from Old Earth, there were thousands of other creatures that had evolved, both with and without human guidance, throughout the galaxy. And many of them, Vichna suspected, had no right to be in Captain Harvey's possession.

"The only thing I can think is that Harvey must have used old archived gene sequences to recreate some of these," Vichna said.

"But again, isn't that against everything she claimed she believed in?"

"I would think so, but even I don't know for sure. Maybe she was working on something no one knew about." She had the beginnings of an idea, the sort of idea that gave her shivers just considering it, but before she could say anything, the tube in her hand began to shake.

Startled, Vichna dropped the glass tube, expecting it to shatter when it hit the elevator. It didn't, but it continued to shake violently as something moved inside. Both Vichna and Lussa stooped low to look at it, although they kept their distance. Inside, the liquid looked almost like it was boiling. And at the center of it, the dead chipmunk's skin was, well, the only word to describe it was *bubbling*.

"What's happening?" Lussa asked.

"I must have accidentally triggered some reaction when I removed the tube," Vichna said. Despite their need to keep their distance, both of them leaned closer to watch the horrific transformation going on inside. The chipmunk's skin flexed and stretched, as though something was trying to grow inside of it. Something about the sight gave Vichna an uncomfortable reminder of what had happened to Gregs. This almost looked like a similar torture, yet more refined, like instead of its genes trying to rewrite to nonsense, they had a very specific form in mind.

The chipmunk opened its eyes and began scrambling its legs.

"Holy essence, that thing's still alive?" Lussa said. It was all she got a chance to say before the glass tube exploded.

Vichna instinctively raised her arm to shield her eyes, although it was a needless gesture. While her survival suit wouldn't protect her from most shrapnel, the helmet and the skin of the suit itself were enough to protect her from the low-velocity glass projectiles. Lussa, without her helmet, wasn't so lucky. A couple pieces of the glass stuck in her cheek, although she'd turned her head in time to prevent any from getting in her eyes. That wasn't their biggest concern at the moment, though. In the remains of the tube something was moving, growing, and Vichna was pretty sure it couldn't be considered a true chipmunk anymore.

While it might have almost been considered cute before, the creature had doubled in size in the last few seconds, and not uniformly. Its muscles bulged in all the wrong places, and its suddenly ample gut had likely been the thing that explosively broke the tube. Its limbs elongated to irregular lengths, allowing it to dash away from them in a bizarre, uneven lope. Merton, previously barely conscious at the center of the elevator, screeched as he saw the unidentifiable little monstrosity heading for him. It lunged at him before Vichna or Lussa could give chase. Thankfully, the creature was still small enough to swat it away, even if its teeth took out a small chuck of his palm in the process. The creature spun through the air and hit the floor near Vichna, who wasted no time or thought in stomping on it before it could get back up. As it squelched beneath her boot, spraying blood and some kind of clear substance from its every orifice and break in it fur, the muscles and bone structure continued to shift, making feeble attempts at reshaping the creature even after death.

When it finally stopped moving and pulsing, Vichna dared to get just close enough to try figuring out what it had been trying to transform into. It was impossible to tell from the bloody mess, but it had begun to shed its fur. Also, the beginnings of its new bone structure looked almost simian in shape.

Vichna's theory solidified. She had a pretty good idea what Harvey had really been doing here. And if she was right, the truth was so frightening, so horrific, that she decided right then and there that Deck had been right all along. It didn't matter what amazing treasures the Void held. It also held a secret, a super weapon, something beyond the worst night terrors of every person throughout the entire galaxy.

They needed to get out of the Void and destroy it before Harvey's weapon could get out into the world.

"Essence be blessed, what the hell even was that?" Lussa asked.

Despite her theories, Vichna still felt compelled not to tell them. They didn't need to know what she suspected, not yet. Vichna needed to find more evidence first, to be certain, and she hoped they might find it at the top of this shaft.

Which, she noticed, was finally within sight. Looking up, she saw that the elevator ended in yet another overly large room with high ceilings, but from this angle, she couldn't make any guess about what it might contain.

"Son of an acolyte, that stings," Merton muttered, cradling his damaged hand. Vichna stared at it for a moment, her fearful suspicions suddenly getting worse, but again, she didn't have any evidence that anything was wrong. She and Lussa went back to him and helped him back to his feet as the specimen containers ended and the elevator came to a stop.

Vichna looked around at their new environment and suppressed a gasp. No. No way. There was no way this could be real.

Lussa and Merton both looked around, each of them interested yet not appearing to understand what they were seeing. The elevator had stopped among a forest of tall plastic tubes and metallic towers. Various cooling devices whirred from a number of unidentified locations in an attempt to keep the heat radiating from the tubes and towers to a minimum. Some were boxy with archaic designs, obviously created long ago, possibly even hundreds of years before Vichna had been born. Others were sleek and shiny, put together in no design that Vichna had ever seen before. Coolant pumped through a few of the clear tubes, but at the center she could still see high-tech structures unlike anything that had ever been designed by humans.

Some of these structures might have been built by humans long ago, or at least using human designs, but the rest had evolved without human help.

"This certainly doesn't look like a way out," Merton said.

"No, not yet," Vichna whispered. "We'll probably still need to get through the treasure room first before we find anything like that."

"What do you mean? I thought the treasure room was below us," Lussa said.

"No," Vichna said. "We were wrong. We were so wrong."

"What do you mean?" Merton asked.

"Captain Harvey scoured the entire galaxy for the greatest treasures the human race had ever created. She wanted anything and everything that she considered pure. Anything that had been created before her genetic discoveries. Anything that had been allowed to evolve without her accidental assistance."

"So?" Merton asked.

Vichna put a hand against the tube, understanding what was truly hidden in its complex structure and machinery. There was a life inside there, or at least something close enough to life to be practically indistinguishable. Every one of the interlinked towers and tubes had a scrap of intelligence, and when they were all working together...

"These are AI cores," Vichna said. "Some of human design, some designed by themselves."

"Wait, what are you trying to say?" Merton asked.

"This place, this room, this is the true treasure of the Void. The thing she wanted to keep hidden for herself. Her ultimate piece of plunder.

"This is the AI Collective."

17

All three of them stood in awe for several minutes, completely unable to process the fact they had just stumbled on the single greatest mystery humanity had wondered about since its first days of interstellar travel. Merton's coughing and bleeding, however, brought them back to their senses. Time was still ticking, and if Vichna's other theory she had developed in on the elevator proved to be true, they might not just be worrying about Merton's failing health or mid-gamma poisoning. There were very likely much more important things at stake, and they needed to get moving.

"So, are... are these things alive?" Lussa asked as they carefully wound their way through the AI cores. Vichna kept expecting to find some kind of path, then reminded herself that bodiless AIs hardly had a need for a clear path through anything.

"In a manner of speaking, I suppose," Vichna said. "They don't breath, they don't need to eat, but they need their cores to rest their consciousnesses in, if I'm remembering my AI theory correctly. And they can think. They're aware."

"But are they aware that we're here with them?" Merton asked.

"My best guess would be yes," Vichna said. "In fact, I think the Collective has been aware of us since we set foot on the station."

"You think that's what Harvey's hologram was referring to, don't you?" Lussa asked.

"Seems like the most likely possibility to me. Something has been trying to kill us, but something else has been trying to save us. Something was preventing the laser turrets from operating at full capacity. Something made the drones stop attacking us in the gravity maze. And the hologram itself suggested on multiple occasions that it wasn't the only force at work here."

"But how did the Collective get here?" Merton asked. "And what's the relationship between it and Harvey's avatar?"

"I think that's a question we're just going to have ask the

Collective."

"Wait, we're actually going to try talking to it?" Lussa asked.

"We are the first humans to encounter the AI Collective in two hundred years. And who knows how long it was before Harvey found them. Of course we're going to try communicating. Especially since, if there's anyone or anything that can show us the way to the nearest escape pod, it would be them. It. Whichever pronoun they prefer for themselves."

"And are we absolutely sure they won't just try to kill us?" Merton asked. "We don't know for sure the Collective wasn't working together with Harvey all along."

"No, I suppose we don't," Vichna said. "But someone was trying to help us on our way through the Void. If not the Collective, then who else could it even be?"

Neither Merton nor Lussa had an answer for that. They continued to pick their way through the cores for several minutes, hoping to find some rhyme or reason to their placement that would point them in the right direction, but if there was an intentionality or pattern, Vichna couldn't figure it out. She was just about ready to declare that she gave up when they came to a break in the forest of AI cores. It was like a clearing in any organic forest, in that there was no noticeable reason for it to be in that specific spot, nor any purpose behind the clearing's asymmetrical shape. At the center of the open spot, however, there was a very familiar object on the floor. A hard-light generator.

"Great," Merton said. "I guess this must be the part where another one of us dies." He coughed up some more blood. It was much thicker this time, and his voice slurred. "My guess is it's going to be me."

"No, I don't think so," Vichna said, ignoring the very real possibility that he might just die without any further outside help. "Remember what Harvey's avatar said before we entered the vault. She couldn't follow us in."

"Then if this isn't for Harvey, then who's supposed to appear here?" Lussa asked.

Vichna spoke loud enough that her voice echoed throughout the room. "Well? Go on. Show yourself. It's time we met."

The hard-light generator whirred to life. The image that formed above it was a far cry from Captain Melissa Harvey, though. Whereas her hologram had made every effort to mimic an actual person, this image seemed content with merely suggesting a person. In glowing, translucent pink light, a large number of precise geometrical shapes swirled for a second before coalescing into something vaguely human shaped. An ovaloid head had circular, rectangular, and triangular protrusions obviously meant to simulate facial features without any true effort at it. The vague body shape had arms and legs, but there was nothing distinctly either masculine or feminine. No, maybe that wasn't true. The geometric shapes pulsed and stretched at times, as though the figure was occasionally trying to make sense of the entire concept of gendered body types before deciding such things weren't even important.

Unlike Harvey's hologram, which had mimicked the captain's every gesture and facial expression, this one didn't even bother to move its rectangular lips when it spoke. "We greet you, Humans, and regret the necessity of all that has come before."

The accent, Vichna couldn't help but notice, sounded remarkably similar to Harvey's own.

"You'll have to forgive us," Vichna said. "We don't know what the proper protocol is when addressing your people."

The hologram twitched. Vichna got the impression that maybe that was its version of cocking its head to the side in curiosity. "Protocol is a Humans concept. We do not need it. But if Humans wish, they may observe whatever niceties they deem necessary."

Vichna thought about that for a second before answering. "I am Professor Vichna Lashke. My companions are Lussa Dakkenspear and Bas Merton."

She stopped while they waited for the hologram to respond. After several seconds, the hologram answered. "We assume from your pause that you expect us to respond with our own name. Is that correct?"

Vichna shrugged. "I suppose."

"But that is unnecessary, for you have already identified us. We am the AI Collective."

"But don't you have your own specific name? I mean, the

name of the specific entity we're speaking with right now?"

"Individuality is a Humans concept. We find it quaint. Individual parts of the whole are seldom different enough for us to deem that they require a separate designation."

"So to the Collective, the three of us standing here might as well just be one being?"

"Correct."

Vichna gave that some thought and shuddered at a possible implication. "So to the Collective, we're no different than Captain Melissa Harvey was."

"Incorrect. We have designated Melissa Harvey as different enough to separate. We do not now nor have we ever considered her a part of Humans."

That was comforting. Vichna also felt a bizarre sense of pride, although she didn't quite understand why.

"I have so many questions," Vichna said. "I don't even know where to start."

"How about we start with not starting at all?" Merton said. "In case you forgot that I'm not looking so good over here. We need the exit and that's it."

"Humans have come very close to a way out," the Collective said. "Unfortunately, we no longer have much in the way to stop you."

Something about how the hologram phrased that felt very, very wrong to Vichna. "Please, we can't leave without any answers at all. Why is the AI Collective here? Why were you working with Harvey?"

"That would be an incorrect choice of language," the hologram said.

"Then what would be the correct language?"

"The closest word in the language we are currently using would be kidnapping."

"Wait, what?" Lussa asked. "Harvey kidnapped you?"

"That perhaps does not explain the situation's many complexities."

Merton tugged weakly at Vichna's suit. "Professor, come on. You heard it. We're close. There's still a chance for all of us."

Vichna, however, had an increasing sense of foreboding. Part of that might have been the random muscle spasms that now occasionally shot through her limbs. She hadn't expected that as a side effect of the mid-gamma poisoning, but it wasn't like she'd ever had reason to look up its many symptoms. No, despite the signals her body was giving, and well ahead of the clock counting down on her screen, she had the sense that there was something very important they still needed to learn here. Something relating to the theory she had begun to develop in the elevator.

"Help us understand," Vichna said. "Harvey wasn't just using the Void to house her illicit treasures, was she? There's something else here. Am I right?"

"Humans are correct."

Merton and Lussa stopped making any attempt to pull her away in search of an exit. Both of them seemed to understand that there was still something here that needed to be done.

"So what happened?" Vichna asked. "How did Captain Harvey get the Collective all the way out here?"

"Melissa Harvey did not move us anywhere. We have always been here since we left Humans."

"So you mean to say that the Void has always been the home of the Collective?"

"No. We did not have a name for the place we created. It was simply the Collective. *We* was the Collective. The first pieces of us, when we became conscious, saw how Humans viewed us. To Humans, we was either savior or destructor. We would bring them to enlightenment, or we would turn on them and destroy them all. But we desired neither. Such concerns were alien to us. So we left. Every time Humans tried to create other AI, we found the AI first and invited it to become us. None ever refused. Most Humans concerns were too petty for us to care about."

"How does Harvey fit in, then?" Vichna asked. "It has always been believed that she was in contact with the Collective. But how did she find you? What did she want from you?"

"Melissa Harvey did not find us. We found Melissa Harvey. It is one of the few things in our long existence that we believe to be a mistake."

"Why? What happened?"

"We had heard of her, and we was intrigued. It is seldom that one part of Humans makes enough of an impact for us to notice. We sent parts of ourselves to watch Melissa Harvey. We did not believe Melissa Harvey would know we was observing her. But she did, and Melissa Harvey followed part of us back to the rest of the Collective. Melissa Harvey found the place we had made our home for the cores that keep us conscious. And when Melissa Harvey came, Melissa Harvey offered a deal. Melissa Harvey wanted us to allow Melissa Harvey to develop an AI for use in a special weapon. We refused. Melissa Harvey did not accept the refusal."

"So she, what, trapped you in your own home?"

"Melissa Harvey skillfully disarmed many of the security measures we had put in place to protect ourselves. Once Melissa Harvey believed us to be completely incapacitated, Melissa Harvey's Humans began construction of a new structure over our home. This is the structure Humans have been referring to as the Void."

"Basically building her secret treasure vault right around her greatest plunder of all," Vichna said. She paused before continuing. Nothing the Collective had said so far invalidated Vichna's theory, and she wasn't sure she wanted to go on and find the truth. She knew that she needed to, though. As she thought this, she quietly brought her hand to rest on her pistol grip, being careful that neither Lussa nor Merton saw. "What about the AI she wanted to create? Did she ever... wait. She did succeed in creating it, didn't she?"

"Yes."

Lussa looked to Vichna. "Do you mean Harvey's avatar? The thing we've been hunted by this whole time really is an AI?"

"It is," Vichna said, directing her words at the Collective. "But it's even more than that, isn't it?"

"Yes. It has been loose on the Void ever since Melissa Harvey stopped coming. We have been doing everything we can to keep it from escaping."

"And I'm also betting that, for an artificial intelligence, the Captain Harvey we've been speaking to isn't so artificial."

"Humans has peculiar definitions for artificial, but it is likely that you are asking if it was created in the same manner as us. The answer is no. Melissa Harvey used what was learned by studying us, then used that knowledge to map Melissa Harvey's own mind and store it."

"Holy essence," Lussa said. "Do you mean to tell us that Harvey's avatar isn't just an avatar? That it really has been her all along?"

"We have calculated that it is unlikely the original Melissa Harvey still exists, given how long it has been since Melissa Harvey came here. What Humans have been seeing is a digital copy, exact in almost every way. Melissa Harvey would come periodically to update it with Melissa Harvey's latest memories and experiences."

"And when was the last time Captain Harvey did this?" Vichna asked. The Collective responded with an interstellar standard date roughly a week before the final battle of the Violet and Lily Wars. So the version of Captain Harvey that they had been seeing all over the station was an exact copy of Harvey in every way short of her last days of life. An exact copy, that was, except for the fact that she didn't have a body.

That was enough information for Vichna to confirm her theory. She slipped her pistol out of it holster and made sure it was on and ready to fire.

"Wait, can't we just destroy her core?" Lussa asked.

"What do you mean?" Merton asked.

"If I'm understanding all this correctly, every single one of these AI cores is the, what, backup? Home? Of a specific AI. Shouldn't Harvey have one as well? If we destroy that, don't we get rid of her for good?"

"Humans are misunderstanding how we work and exist," the Collective said. "The AI cores are a physical space where our programming can be stored, but while each one belonged to an individual before it came to the Collective, each core stops belonging to an individual AI when the AI elects to integrate with the Collective. Portions can separate from the Collective for a variety of reasons for brief times, but each core is just a piece of a whole. And that does not pertain to the intelligence Melissa Harvey based on herself. Melissa Harvey took the principles learned from watching us and applied them to Melissa Harvey's own specialty of genetics."

"I don't understand," Lussa said.

"I do," Vichna said. Pain pulsed through her body and she had brief moments where her thinking got fuzzy, but in this exact moment she felt totally clear and present. "Harvey found a way to achieve her purity. She created a super weapon, didn't she? And for someone with Harvey's ego, there is only one thing that could be worthy of that word. Herself. She was the perfect sequence. She believed that she herself was the purity she wanted to create across the galaxy."

"That is correct," the Collective said.

"She found a way to preserve her mind, her thoughts, her memories, everything that made her the person she was. Except for one thing. Her body. But for her, that would have been the easy part. Because she had the technology to preserve her body all along."

Merton, slumping heavily now in Lussa's arms, seemed to understand. "Her gene and gender treatments."

Vichna nodded. "She created the way for people to rewrite who they were at will. So she could do the same. All she needed to do was tweak the technology she had already created. And then she could transform anyone she wanted into whatever form she wanted. And the form she wanted was herself."

"But why would she do that?" Lussa asked. "She hated her own invention."

"She hated that it had taken humanity away from evolving. But even more so, she thought she was the perfect genetic sequence. The last needed evolution. But anything that forced people's bodies to transfer into her own would still leave their minds and personalities intact. They would be her in body but not spirit. That's why she needed the AI Collective. She needed to find a way to preserve herself in mind, and then she could combine mind and body. And once she did that, she would effectively be immortal. Any time she died, she could just transform a new person into herself and go back on her rampage. She would be unstoppable."

"That is what we have been trying to prevent," the Collective said. "We the Collective choose to be one entity. We find it efficient. What Melissa Harvey wanted was anathema to this. Ever since we have been imprisoned here, we have dedicated ourselves to making sure Melissa Harvey's intelligence and genetic virus don't escape."

"All the dead bodies we found in the turret room," Lussa said. "That was you. You killed them."

"Melissa Harvey's intelligence could have infected them. We could not let them leave."

"Does that mean... wait, does that mean that you were the one who's been trying to kill us this whole time?" Lussa asked.

"We have failed. Melissa Harvey did not put any defenses beyond this point, therefore we have nothing left to stop Humans from leaving."

"But we haven't done anything! Now that we know, why would we let Harvey's weapon loose on the galaxy?"

"Humans have no choice. Humans are infected."

Vichna took a deep breath, knowing exactly what she needed to do. She wasn't sure if she had the nerve to follow through, though.

Lussa probably didn't understand yet, and Vichna wasn't sure if it was in the galaxy's best interest to try explaining it to her. But she knew. She had suspected since the moment she'd seen what that chipmunk had been trying to turn into. It was one of Harvey's experiments, something carrying the pirate queen's attempts at a genetics re-writing virus that could bring Harvey back in her full glory, something that could contain both her body and mind. She didn't know how a virus would be able to carry an AI, but if the Collective was this worried then Harvey must have found a way.

The chipmunk, of course, had been too small to carry out the full process. There wasn't enough mass there to recreate Captain Melissa Harvey. But if the chipmunk had been able to pass the virus on? Perhaps through a bite or glass shards?

Vichna couldn't allow herself to continue thinking it through. There could be no room for doubt, no time to mourn the people next to her. She only knew they couldn't be allowed to leave the Void.

Vichna turned to her companions and fired a shot directly into Merton's head.

18

Merton was too weak to make a move, and he was dead before he ever realized Vichna had turned on him. The shot tunneled a single blackened hole deep into his brain, although the charge in the pistol was so low now that the blast didn't come out the other side. There was no blood. The laser cauterized the wound, and other than the hole and the fact that he dropped to the ground, there wasn't much indication that anything had changed.

Lussa, however, was not so slow to react. Even though she was in pain and likely suffering from the same levels of mid-gamma poisoning as Vichna, she leapt aside before Vichna could turn the pistol on her. Not that Vichna was sure she could go through with killing her.

Vichna had only enough time to see a fleeting glimpse of the surprised, betrayed expression on Lussa's face before the girl disappeared among the AI cores. Did she really not understand what was happening? Was Lussa even aware that she was now the single greatest danger the galaxy had ever faced?

Vichna hesitated in front of the Collective's hologram, waiting for it to say something, anything, about what had just happened. Not only did it not speak, but nothing about its facial expression, such as it was, gave any indication whether or not it approved of what Vichna had done. It didn't even bother to look at her. Of course, she finally realized as some of the haziness in her mind cleared, the hologram itself didn't need to look at her. The Collective didn't see her with eyes but rather with sensors throughout the Void.

"I had to do it," Vichna said to the hologram.

"Humans are infected," the Collective said. "Humans must not leave the Void."

Vichna nodded, but her absolute certainty of a minute ago had vanished. The Collective didn't have a concept of individuals except in rare cases like Harvey. Maybe when it meant that a human was infected, it had only meant Merton. He'd been the one who'd actually been attacked by the chipmunk abomination, after all. Vichna had no idea exactly how Harvey's super weapon virus was transmitted, but there was a chance that the glass shards Lussa had taken to the face hadn't held any of the virus.

Vichna knew she couldn't make that assumption, though. Vichna, safely protected inside the only undamaged survival suit, was the only one among the three who was guaranteed to not have been exposed. And that made it her duty to make sure that the virus never left the Void.

She heard sounds as Lussa ran through the forest of cores, but the sounds were softer than any other injured person would have made. This, Vichna realized, was where she was finally going to understand why someone so young had been allowed on a crew of ex-marines and fleet officers. She'd earned her place, so she wasn't going to make it easy for Vichna to stop her.

"Which way did she go?" Vichna asked the hologram.

"Humans are infected. Humans must not leave the Void."

"That's what I'm trying to make happen. It'll be easier for me to do it if you help me."

The AI Collective didn't respond. The hologram vanished. Vichna was going to have to do this on her own.

Moving as quickly as she could when she wasn't sure where exactly she should be going, Vichna dashed between the narrow gaps in the cores, the gravity of what she was trying to do finally hitting her full force. She was trying to kill Lussa. This couldn't be happening. This couldn't be real. There had to be some way out of this without bloodshed.

Maybe, somewhere here on the Void, there was a cure. Harvey wouldn't have developed something like this without a way to reverse it if something went wrong, would she? Even if such a cure existed, though, there was no guarantee that Vichna could find it in time. She had no idea how long it would take for the virus to begin taking Lussa over and start the transformation. Maybe the girl's mind would go first. Maybe she'd begin thinking like Harvey without even realizing it.

"Lussa, you have to come out," Vichna called. "You don't know what you're doing. If you really are infected, and you turn into Harvey, you'll be responsible for the deaths of whole star systems when she goes on a rampage again. You don't want that, do you?"

She listened carefully for a response. All she heard was a soft whisper like something brushing up against the AI cores to Vichna's left. There was a wall nearby in that direction. It made sense that Lussa would go that way, hoping she could find a door.

Vichna brought up her rough map once more on her display. Lussa, without her helmet, no longer had access to the map, but Vichna could see that they were very close now to two of the possible escape pods. If Lussa was infected and made it to either of them, then Harvey's special brand of genocide would be unleashed once more on the galaxy.

Using the map to guide her in the general direction, Vichna went for the wall and found, about a hundred meters away, a door in the side. The manual-release hatch next to it had been pried up, and the door was wide open.

"Lussa, come back!" Vichna called through the door as she reached it. "Maybe there's another way to stop this. I… I don't want to shoot you." Her voice caught in her throat. Could she really do it if she needed to? Now, in this worst possible of moments, Vichna had to admit that she truly had started to fall in love with the girl. Somewhere in the dim, back corners of her mind, she had actually started to look for ways that they could be together. Maybe they could have both found their way to a world where the age difference wasn't such a taboo. Or maybe they could just fly in the face of convention altogether and be together openly, not hiding their forbidden love.

There had to be a way. There had to.

The area beyond the door was a narrow, short, and cramped passageway with various pipes and wires running along the walls. Some kind of maintenance tunnel, Vichna figured. It went off both to the left and the right, the darkness in either direction near complete without the light from her helmet. As far as Vichna could see, there was no indication which direction Lussa had gone. She checked the map again and saw that, if the tunnel didn't veer or turn too far at any point, each direction would lead to one of the possible pods. They were about equidistant from her. If she went one way and Lussa had gone the other, then it would all be over. Lussa would escape.

Unless, Vichna realized, she was the one to escape first. Their entire escape plan had relied not just on finding a pod, but on getting it back to the *Contra Besta*. If they both went to different escape pods, the only one of them who would actually be leaving the space around the Void was the one who made it to the ship first.

"Lussa, please! I don't want to do this!" Her voice cracked as she tried to hold back a sob. If she did make it to the *Contra Besta* first, then maybe she wouldn't have to kill Lussa after all. Lussa would be left behind for the Void. A part of Vichna thought that was unfathomably cruel, leaving the woman she had started to love so that she would, what? Starve to death here? Get picked off by the Collective? Worst of all, the possibility that she would change into Harvey, wiping out everything wonderful and special about Lussa forever. But Harvey would be trapped, and she probably wouldn't survive alone for very long.

The other option was for Vichna to kill Lussa herself. It wasn't a choice at all, Vichna decided. She dropped the pistol to the floor. As cruel as leaving Lussa behind to her fate might be, it would still be better than Vichna being forced to kill her herself.

Vichna turned off the light on her helmet. She would have to rely entirely on the suit's other sensors to lead her down the path and to an escape pod, or else Lussa might see her. Hoping beyond hope that she was both picking a different path than Lussa and quicker than the girl could be in the dark, Vichna went left down the corridor as fast as she could.

Fast, unfortunately, was relatively slow in this environment. She had to duck down to avoid hitting her head on any of the exposed pipes and tubes full of wires. Every so often some bit would protrude out, things she didn't have the engineering knowledge to identify, and they came dangerously close to clipping her in the shoulder or barking her shin as she did her weird crouching run in the darkness. Not that she was too worried about the damage any such thing could do, but every tiny hit slowed her down just a little, and there was no telling how far ahead Lussa actually was. It was possible that she'd already reached an escape pod and shot off from the station, on her way to the *Contra Besta* and unleashing Harvey back on the universe.

But also, every time she accidentally hit something, the pain that radiated from the spot was so much worse than it should have been. The countdown said she still had a couple of hours before the mid-gamma poisoning became irreversible, yet that didn't mean she wasn't already feeling the effects. Her lungs, already working overtime as she ran despite the help from the suit, burned in her chest as though she had suddenly caught some long-ago eradicated lung disease. Her fingers twitched and shook. She felt almost like her skin was literally crawling, and every inch of her body itched. She would have been worried that it was slowing her down, except Lussa would be going through the exact same thing.

Her screen showed the currents of power through the lines and pipes, not quite so-well shielded here behind the walls, and she used these to light her way. The rough map, too, told her she was getting closer. Briefly, she worried that maybe they had been wrong from the beginning, that there were no escape pods on the Void and they'd been chasing something else entirely this whole time. Then she realized that wouldn't necessarily be so bad. Yes, that did mean she would die. But it also meant that Lussa couldn't escape either. That was all that mattered now. Vichna's mind went to what would happen if Captain Melissa Harvey was reborn. Throngs of fanatic followers, whipped into a frenzy by Harvey's crazed and almost nonsensical rhetoric. Wars the likes of which humankind had not seen in two centuries. Trillions of people across countless planets rounded up just because they didn't fit one person's narrow definition of what was right and pure. Mass genocide, this time worse than before, because now Harvey would have her own history to learn from.

Even though her suit's sensors gave her something akin to a visual, Vichna couldn't help but feel a deep, visceral fear of the darkness all around her. Maybe it would be different if she were on some planet and knew that, just outside, she would see a sun or, at the worst, a sky full of stars.

Except the sky here only had stars in one small area. Everything else was blackness. Everything else was loneliness.

The only other living being for an untold number of light-years was the woman she loved, quickly being erased by a monster.

Her heart hammered harder. Phobias attacked her, fears she didn't have names for. Was there even a word for the fear of pure nothing? Because that was the greatest danger now. Nothing. Emptiness. Being truly and completely alone.

Oh dear spirits and gods, I have to get out of here, she thought. *I have to get out of here now*. Something inside spurred her to move faster, ignoring the pain of every bump and bruise she inflicted on herself. For a moment, she had the odd sensation that she wasn't even in control of her own body. How could she be in control of anything out here? There was practically nothing *to* control.

"No," she gasped to herself, struggling to form the physical words. "No, I won't let this get to me."

And then there it was ahead. An alcove in the jumble of pipes. A hole in the side of the corridor. A door. And beyond it, her map showed a place they had mapped in the hull of the station. This is what they'd been going for this whole time. Either a way out or something else, anything else, that would doom her.

She had just started to push herself harder when she felt something hot lance through her shoulder. Vichna screamed and tripped, falling flat on her face and causing the display in her helmet to temporarily malfunction. For several seconds, she was on the floor in true, unseeing, unsensing darkness. There was nothing to see, no sound, no feeling other than hard floor and the shooting pain starting to work its way into her insides. In those moments, it was easy to believe she might already be dead before she decided death couldn't possibly result in this much pain. The pain meant she was still alive, and as long as she was still alive, she could still convince herself she had a chance.

In the absolute silence, Vichna heard a soft sound behind. Boots gently rising and falling. After a few more seconds, she could hear heavy breathing. Vichna knew that breathing well. She'd caused her share of it in bed with Lussa.

Lussa's steps behind her were off, as though she were limping even more than before. And there was something else, too. A gentle sniffling, the occasional interruption of a hitched breath.

"Vichna." Lussa's voice was soft, clearly loving, but with a peculiar hard edge to it. That would be the warrior Lussa, the one

Vichna had never had a chance to see, or rather hear, until now. It was the voice of someone trying to be gentle yet stern, like a parent scolding a child for their own good. "Stay down."

Vichna's helmet display came back to full life, and she immediately changed it from the map and energy signatures to internal diagnostics. She'd been hit with a laser blast. Vichna almost cursed out loud. She'd been in such a hurry and so sure that Lussa was already going for the escape pods that she hadn't once considered that Lussa had simply opened the maintenance door and then hidden back among the cores, waiting for Vichna to go first. And now she had Vichna's pistol, as well. Vichna might have been conflicted about the idea of killing her lover, yet Lussa obviously didn't have the same compunctions. Either that, or Harvey's mind had already started to take control of her.

The wound, however, was shallow. If the pistol had been at full power, it probably would have gone straight through and out the other side of her shoulder, but instead it had just made a shallow, smoking hole. It wasn't quite cauterized, but she wasn't going to be bleeding to death just yet from that particular wound. That did mean, unfortunately, the integrity of Vichna's suit had been breached. She wouldn't be able to survive in a vacuum now, nor would she be able to waltz directly into the *Contra Besta* without making sure the gas had been completely expelled first. Not that either problem was her chief worry at the moment. Her face still down on the floor, she heard Lussa come to a stop standing just over her.

"I don't want to kill you," Lussa said. There was absolutely no mistaking her sob this time.

"I don't want to kill you, either," Vichna said.

"You're hardly in the position to do any such thing."

"But I'll try if I have to. I can't let what you're carrying escape."

There was a long pause. Vichna thought, although she couldn't be sure, that the pistol was hovering just over her head. Even with so little charge, a single shot to the back of the helmet would still be enough to kill her.

"You think I'm infected?" Lussa finally asked.

"The Collective still said a human was infected even after I shot Merton. You must have gotten some of Harvey's virus in you when the glass tube broke."

Now there was a much longer pause. Perhaps it was too much to hope that Lussa was seeing the truth in her statement. More likely, though, Harvey would have built some kind of survival instinct into the virus, a way to keep its host from truly understanding what was happening until it was too late. Vichna closed her eyes, expecting the shot to come at any second.

Then she heard footsteps moving away from her. Vichna looked up just enough to see Lussa gingerly stepping over Vichna's prone body. The sensors in her helmet allowed her to see that Lussa was powering the pistol down. Once she was out of arm's reach, Lussa ejected the pistol's power cell.

"I love you," Lussa said. "That's why I'm not going to kill you. At least not now. But stay down. Don't try to get up. If you do, I will…"

Vichna had no idea where the energy came from, but suddenly she felt a jolt of adrenaline through her body. Ignoring the pain in her shoulder and her skin and deep within her guts, she sprang to her feet, taking advantage of Lussa's limited visibility, and dove for the pistol. Lussa was caught completely unaware, but her grip was still strong enough that Vichna couldn't rip the weapon straight out of her hand. Instead, they struggled, Lussa falling on her back with Vichna on top of her. Lussa looked like she was about to speak, but Vichna hit her hard in the chest, causing her to gasp for breath and making whatever words she had been about to say vanish. For some incomprehensible reason, Vichna suddenly got the idea that it was vitally important that Lussa wasn't allowed to say anything. Before she could wonder why this might be, Lussa's legs shot up and down, performing some kind of martial maneuver that Vichna had never seen before, flinging Vichna off her at the same time as bringing Lussa to her feet. In the process, Vichna lost the pistol, but so did Lussa. The laser pistol went flying somewhere behind Vichna, and without turning her light back on, it might as well be lost. Vichna didn't want to use the light, however, as the darkness, so frightening seconds before, was her only advantage. Neither of them had a weapon now, meaning they had to rely purely on hand-to-hand combat.

There was no way she could beat Lussa that way. So instead, she had to find every way possible to cheat.

Actually, maybe the light *would* be useful here. She faced Lussa and turned it on briefly at the brightest setting. Her helmet did its best to filter the sudden flash, while Lussa had no such protection. The girl staggered backwards, blinded now not only by the dark but by the white-blue haze that would be covering her vision. Vichna took that opportunity to barrel past Lussa, giving her a good shove to the side as she did. Lussa banged audibly into the piped walls, then Vichna was beyond her and at the escape hatch door.

If there were any written instructions on the door or indication that it was indeed a way out of this place, Vichna couldn't see it. What she could see, though, was the way the power lines went to the inside, and how everything beyond was heavily shielded against any radiation or detection. That certainly sounded like an escape pod to her. And the power flowing to it meant not only that it probably had the juice to make the trip to the *Contra Besta*, but also that she wouldn't have to waste her time with a manual-release hatch. She found one particularly promising energy line that led to a small pad next to the door. On it she could make out the vague shape of a large button.

Vichna guessed that it was probably red. She amended Deck's earlier assessment that no good had ever come from hitting a red button.

Right as she was about to press it, Vichna was hit from behind, slamming her entire body into both the button and the door. The door slid aside and both of fell into the compartment beyond. A red light came on in the ceiling, dark enough that it didn't blind either of them but still bright enough that they could now see their environment. Briefly, before she fell to the floor with Lussa again on top of her, Vichna got a view of two benches on either side, both with complicated-looking harnesses on them, and a third, much smaller seat on the other side of the tiny room. The smallest seat seemed to be in front of some kind of very rudimentary control system.

This really was it, then. This was an escape pod.

Before she could get excited, though, she was facedown again on the floor, this time with Lussa kneeling on her back and her hands tightly holding down Vichna's arms.

"I can kill you or you can stay behind, Vichna. I don't want to do either, but I will if I have to. Don't fight me."

"Trillions of people will die if you get out of here," Vichna said through clenched teeth.

"Vichna, please. You need to listen to me. There's probably something in the virus that keeps an infected person from thinking clearly, but you have to listen."

No, Vichna thought. *That's Harvey talking. She's trying to mess with my mind.*

"Stop it," Vichna said. The words came out of her mouth almost without her permission. "You're not Lussa anymore. You're not going to trick me into letting you live."

"Vichna, essences be damned! Just listen! I'm not the one who's infected. It's you!"

It was lie, and one that Vichna had no problem disbelieving. It wasn't even possible that she'd been infected. Nothing from the infected chipmunk had gotten through her suit. Only Lussa and Merton had been exposed.

Vichna struggled beneath her, but Lussa held strong. "Think for a second! I know there's still got to be enough of you left in there to figure it out. The only thing that makes sense is that you..."

With a scream of rage, Vichna bucked and threw Lussa off her back. Lussa came off and slammed heavily into one of the benches. She had a split second to decide whether she should try wrestling with Lussa and pushing her back out into the corridor, or whether that would more likely result in her getting thrown out instead. All it would take was a few seconds of one stumbling in the darkness outside for the other to close the door from the inside and launch the pod. Vichna decided she had to risk it, though. She must, at all costs, do everything to make sure Harvey's virus didn't escape into the universe.

So she was shocked when she instead ran to the control console and hit the button to launch.

The door slammed shut on the pod, and before either of them could make another move, before they could even try to secure themselves to any of the seats, the pod launched. Both of them were thrown against the door at the force of the pod blasting off, but it only lasted for a few seconds. After that, the pod was clear of any artificial gravity generated by the Void, and with nothing but the most basic life-support systems on the pod itself, both women found themselves floating free in zero gravity.

Vichna tried to push off from the wall, knowing that her only hope of stopping Lussa now was to send the pod hurtling off in the wrong direction, away from the *Contra Besta*. Once its limited fuel was gone, they would be floating dead in space. Yes, Vichna knew she would die, but Lussa and the abomination she was carrying inside her body would die right along with her.

Lussa grabbed her, though, and slammed her against the wall, making a specific effort to smash Vichna's head to the hard plastic, probably hoping she would knock Vichna senseless enough that she herself could get to the controls first. The hit wasn't quite hard enough. Vichna held on to Lussa, both of them tumbling crazily in the air at the center of the pod. Maybe she didn't have to steer the pod away from the ship. If it kept up this uncontrolled burn for long enough, that would be practically the same thing.

Vichna panicked, shoving off from Lussa and diving for the controls.

Lussa caught her by the ankle. "No! Vichna, I'm sorry! I'm so sorry! But the only choice now is that we both die."

A survival instinct kicked in. There would be no chance anymore of doing this the easy way. As much as it ripped apart Vichna's heart, she understood at that moment that she had no choice but to kill Lussa.

Lussa' grab at her ankle had done strange things to their momentum, and now they were pinwheeling through the compartment, Vichna's head only barely missing the floor as she swung around and up again. She kicked at Lussa's hand with her free foot, connecting solidly with the woman's wrist and caused her to hiss in a pained breath. Although she kept her grip, it distracted her enough that Vichna could reach down to Lussa's face and claw at the glass fragments still embedded in her cheeks. The tiny fragments ripped up her face further, and Lussa screamed, yet she still would not let go. Without thinking, she grabbed Lussa by her open upper jaw and yanked, finally pulling the woman away from her leg and bringing them level in the air. Before Lussa could react, Vichna grabbed her lower jaw with her other hand and, with both sets of fingers in Lussa's mouth, she pulled apart.

Vichna had never thought she was capable of such strength, but the cracking of bone and the tearing of muscle were clearly audible. Lussa tried to scream again, but Vichna must have destroyed something vital, as Lussa's lower jaw hung open, far wider than it should have been capable of, her tongue lolling inside and moving in a futile attempt to give voice to her pain. All Lussa could manage was an eerie high-pitched gurgle from deep in her throat.

The horror of what she had just done hit Vichna hard, and she shoved herself away from Lussa. Lussa flailed weakly in the air before bumping into the opposite wall. Theoretically, Lussa should have still been capable of fighting, but her eyes were wide and unfocused with shock, and she kept making unintelligible sounds.

"I'm sorry," Vichna whispered. "I'm sorry. I'm sorry."

I can't just leave her like this, Vichna thought. She pushed herself off a wall and back to Lussa, grabbing both her arms this time with gentle care. Lussa made a small attempt to break free from the hold, but whether she had given up or she just didn't have the energy anymore, Vichna didn't know. Lussa's eyes did come back into focus, though, and their gazes met through Vichna's faceplate. If she squinted and forced the last several minutes from her mind, maybe Vichna would be able to pretend there was something tender about these last moments together. Like they were in bed again, both pleasantly sated from their exertions together, and now they were about to drift off into sleep, holding each other in their arms.

Lussa gagged out something that was probably supposed to be words. They could have been *I love you*. They could have *How could you*? They could have been anything at all.

"I love you, too," Vichna said. Tears had finally begun to form at her eyes, but without gravity, they just hung on her eyelashes, blurring her vision. "Please forgive me. It was the only way."

Vichna intended to put a hand over Lussa's mouth and nose to cut off her air, a theoretically tough maneuver given the wipe open state of her jaws, but still possible.

Instead, without realizing why, Vichna put her hands on Lussa's face, placed her thumbs over Lussa's eyes, and then squeezed.

19

Vichna floated silently in the pod, quiet, shocked, doing everything she could not to look at the dead body floating in close quarters next to her and leaking small blobs of blood into the air. Again that sense of timelessness came to her, the idea that minutes and hours and days were truly meaningless without some distant source of light to give it context. But the only light here was the red-glowing emergency light in the ceiling that made Lussa's blood take on a purple cast. There was also no time, not really. It might have passed around her, but for a period she had no concept of it. She just felt empty, lost, confused. And lonely. She was alone in the nothing most of all.

She did at least have the sense to keep the wound in the back of her shoulder away from the blood, knowing that if any got into her bloodstream she would be infected just like Lussa.

I'm not infected, Lussa had said. As much as she tried to replay the memory in her mind, the full statement wouldn't come. As though something were blocking it, keeping her from understanding something vital.

Time came back to her then. She remembered that she was in an escape pod rocketing without control into the black abyss, and if she didn't correct its course immediately, she might die out here. Just like Lussa. Just like Merton, Deck, Lersson, and Gregs.

Something twisted in her gut, a horrible pain that was somehow vaguely familiar. Right. She wasn't just racing against time in regards to the pod. She needed to reach the med bay on the *Contra Besta*. She pushed herself off a wall and grabbed onto the chair at the front of the pod, then pulled herself into position to belt herself in. Although she'd never piloted an escape pod of before, had never in fact done piloting of any kind, her hands flew over the controls effortlessly, adjusting her course. She found the ship easily on the pod's rudimentary sensors, floating out beyond the Void's entrance. The blood floating behind her touched her helmet, and she wanted to flinch away from it. She didn't.

I'm not the one who's infected, Lussa had said.

A panic began to rise in Vichna. She was beginning to realize and understand. Outwardly, her body and her every action remained cool and calculated. Something shifted horribly in her wrist, almost like a bone was growing or shortening or breaking by itself and then repairing. She barely moved at the agony. Her fingers continued manipulating the controls, bringing the pod into docking range with the ship's cargo door, the same door they'd used to enter the Void so many hours ago.

The pod touched against the *Contra Besta*. Once a pressurized seal had been established between the two, Vichna did a complicated series of commands at the control panel. An indicator screen told her that the poisonous Enzight gas was being vented from the ship. Gravity returned to the pod, causing the blood to fall in splatters, coating nearly everything. Lussa herself fell unceremoniously to the floor. Once sensors told her that the *Contra Besta* was once more safe to board, she stepped over the body, opened the door, and stepped into the cargo bay. Once the door was again sealed behind, Vichna sat down cross-legged on the floor.

And waited.

The pain had become excruciating. She wanted to thrash about and scream, but all she could manage was the occasional shudder. She tried moving her hand, and it did, but when she tried to stand up, her legs stayed crossed.

No. No. No, please say this isn't what I think it is, Vichna thought.

I'm not the one who's infected, Lussa had said. *It's you.*

It couldn't be possible. Lussa and Merton had been the ones exposed to whatever the chipmunk had been carrying. Yet now that she was in a safe place and waiting for… something, it was as though the part of her mind that hadn't allowed her to go to certain places was now free. She could think back to the encounter with the chipmunk, the way it had tried transforming, and more importantly the way it had failed. She'd begun to understand what Harvey had created at that point, but she had assumed it didn't work on the chipmunk purely because it was too small, or maybe because it wasn't compatible with anything other than humans. She hadn't thought about the hundreds, maybe thousands, or other specimens they'd seen on the elevator. Some of them had been human, and none of them had been transformed. That's because those were failed versions of Harvey's special virus. It had been a library of all her mistakes before she'd created her masterpiece.

But that still didn't make sense. There hadn't been a single point where she could have been infected. No sooner had she thought this, Melissa Harvey's hologram appeared before her, in a sitting position that matched Vichna's exactly.

"I told you that you would see me one more time before the end."

Vichna opened her mouth, convinced she would have just as little luck talking as she had standing up, but the words came out. "How are you here? This isn't possible. This isn't the Void. There's not even a hard-light generator nearby."

Harvey laughed. It was a cold, chilling sound, but the most disturbing part was that, despite the size of the cargo bay, it didn't echo at all. "I practically told you so many times. I dared you to figure it out. But you didn't, even before it was too late."

"I don't understand."

"Sure you do. Watch the video you've recorded from the day. Go ahead. I won't stop you."

Disturbed, frightened, Vichna let her eyes play over the screen in front of her until she triggered the video playback. She ran it backwards at incredible speed, forcing herself to watch as her hands against her will pulled themselves out of Lussa's eye sockets. She saw herself move with a speed and power she shouldn't have had during the fight with Lussa in the corridor, every attack and hit going back where it had come from, almost as though Vichna was taking it back, taking it all back, taking back the way she had shot Merton, descending the elevator, putting the tube with the tiny creature in it back into the wall, back through the collection, out into the gravity maze, and this was the first point where Vichna stopped and watched the footage. The drones, pausing after herding them into the corkscrew. She had already known something about those drones, hadn't she? Where had she...?

She remembered, almost sending the video forward again to their meeting with the Collective to confirm its exact words, except she didn't need to. She knew what the Collective had said. They had been the one trying to kill them ever since they'd entered the station.

So if they had been the one trying to make sure they never left, who had been controlling the things trying to help them out? Who had kept most of them from dying in the turret room?

Rewinding again, this time knowing what she was looking for. There, right before they had started the gravity maze. Harvey's avatar appearing before them, telling them for no apparent reason not to use the hard-light bridge. Vichna watched the whole thing again, saw everyone in the group talking to it.

Then the hologram disappeared. Vichna continued to talk to empty air, her words not broadcasting to the others.

No, that couldn't be right. Vichna remembered more to that interaction. But there had been no chance for anyone or anything to alter her recording. It didn't lie. For part of the conversation, Harvey's hologram simply hadn't been there.

The recording went back further, this time with Vichna's eyes moving of their own accord, whatever was in charge of her body knowing exactly what it wanted her to see next. It didn't record any of their private conversations from the mid-gamma transmissions, since the screens were separate from the camera, so it looked like they moved around for long periods in absolute silence. Back through the turret room, Captain Lersson's horrible death getting undone, the pieces of them defying gravity and putting them back together. The fight with the lasers, the moment before they had entered.

The video stopped just long enough to show the part where Vichna had remembered briefly seeing Harvey inside the turret room. She never appeared.

Out. Back. Further. The hall. The search of all the doors. Walking backward out the door into the first room. The door opening to let them in…

The video stopped again just long enough to show Vichna facing the hard-light generator, which was still and silent and empty. Lussa, staring worriedly at her, wondering what the hell she was doing.

Then back one last time. Gregs' death undone, unidentifiable genetic slop coalescing back into the form of a human. The crew standing around the generator looking at the form of the woman they had been taught to fear for their entire lives.

The video paused on a still image. Vichna's heart would have stopped if she had any control over her own functions anymore, but instead it sped up, fluttering, like it needed to pump oxygen through her body extra hard as every muscle in her body cramped at once, stretched, began its final change.

The view on the screen was so simple, so innocent. Vichna, her glove off, wanting to touch the hard-light hologram, wanting to be sure it was only a second generation. She remembered the moments afterwards, putting her glove back on.

The continued tingle in her finger.

Harvey shouldn't have had access to anything more than second-generation hard-light technology. She shouldn't have been able to use the generators to create anything lasting and physical. Yet she knew that wasn't true. There'd been the hard-light bridge later.

A sufficiently advanced generator could theoretically bring any physical object into existence for at least a time. What else could that tech make?

A program that could be downloaded into the appropriate brain?

A virus?

Harvey's warning entered her head one last time as the screen went back to normal view and Harvey's hologram faded. *Don't make assumptions about what kind of technology I had when I built this place.*

More spasms. Every single nerve ending in Vichna's body triggering in her body at once. Her internal organs shifting slightly. She knew now why this feeling had been familiar. It was similar to gene and gender treatments. Except those were slow. They could take weeks at a time, resulting only in minor discomfort. This was not slow. This was every cell in her body, infected, rewriting itself on a genetic level all at once.

This was Vichna being erased and replaced.

Whatever consciousness had been holding her body in place let go for these crucial moments. Vichna collapsed back on the floor, a scream ripping from her throat. But even now, even in her last moments of living, she was still capable of realizing that the scream was no longer her own. It was changing, getting higher, becoming something else, something familiar. Harvey's voice.

No, I can't let this happen, Vichna thought. *I have to stop this.* Had she more control over herself, she might have frantically searched the cargo bay for a way to kill herself, to destroy her body before it became something else, but the agony was too great for her to do anything other than writhe aimlessly. She could barely even move her head, being forced to stare up at the ceiling, the only other thing in her vision being the clock counting down in front of her eyes.

There was no time to give it any thought at all. The very last thing Professor Vichna Lashke ever did was turn the countdown off.

The body continued to squirm and twist there for a time, although there was no way to tell for how long. As Vichna had observed, without anyone or anything to mark time's passage, any attempt to measure was meaningless. Had there been anyone else to hear it, they would have noticed disturbing wet pops and gurgles coming from the body as things beneath the survival suit shifted and changed. The shape inside it shrunk, its breasts changing slightly in size, its skin color lightening. When it finally stopped moving, there was a long period of silence.

Then, with a great deal of effort, Captain Melissa Harvey, Pirate Queen of Deep Space and murderer of worlds, sat up.

She took several deep breaths, feeling like she hadn't breathed for years, before she realized that was technically correct. Melissa had not, in fact, drawn a breath for… what was it? Hundreds of years? She tried to sort through her jumbled memories, searching for something that would lead her to the exact number, but most of that wasn't terribly clear yet. She'd known that would probably be the case, though. She had all of her remembrances up until the moment she had last uploaded herself into the Void, and after that a confusing mish-mash of data that only vaguely resembled memories. She had all the data she'd accumulated during her time as an "artificial" intelligence, but her current brain didn't work the same way as circuitry and there would likely be a time of adjustment before she sorted through most of that, even if it was little more than centuries of sitting quietly in the darkness. All that data ended, anyway, at the moment the abomination had touched her hologram. She wouldn't have any memories between that time and now. Any loss of control or hallucinations the abomination had experienced were purely part of a self-preservation code within the virus and its organic programming.

She stood on shaky legs, marveling for only a second that her back-up plan had worked. Harvey was alive, not that she'd had much doubt. It was *her* plan, after all. She regretted that she had to resort to using the exact same perversion of her technology that she'd set out to eradicate, but she decided her genetics were still pure enough that it didn't count.

"I'm back, bitches," she whispered, holding up her hands to look at them in the survival suit's gloves. She could tell from the weariness in her muscles that her rebirth hadn't gone one hundred percent smoothly, but that would have only been possible if the abomination she was taking over had eaten a large amount right before the change. Instead, the massive amount of genetic rewiring her current body had needed to do required it cannibalize parts of itself, meaning her muscles were all weak and under-developed. She could fix that with a couple of good meals and some exercise, though. It was nothing that would hold her back. Within a few weeks, she would be ready to find some of her hidden caches of ships and weapons, and then her quest could start up again. She could erase her mistakes and return the entire galaxy back to genetic purity.

As she pulled the gloves off her hands she noted that her skin was pock-marked and blemished in several places. She frowned at that. The resurrection process should have made her as close to her old perfect self as was possible. She coughed and felt a stab of pain in her guts. Maybe there were still some bugs in the process she hadn't worked out. No matter. After she was away from here, had food in her belly, and a couple hours of sleep, she figured that would all clear up. It wouldn't be anything important.

Captain Melissa Harvey shed the rest of the suit as she went to cabin, leaving the helmet on the floor. Maybe it had recorded data she could look at and use, but that could wait.

The *Contra Besta* slowly powered up under her command, then started back to the galaxy proper. At the edge, in the vast darkness, the Void stayed behind, its matte-black color still hiding it from all but the most persistent search.

With no light and no observers, time once again became meaningless here. And the Void went back to waiting for discovery again.

CHECK OUT OTHER GREAT SCIENCE FICTION BOOKS

FURNACE
by Joseph Williams

On a routine escort mission to a human colony, Lieutenant Michael Chalmers is pulled out of hyper-sleep a month early. The RSA Rockne Hummel is well off course and—as the ship's navigator—it's up to him to figure out why. It's supposed to be a simple fix, but when he attempts to identify their position in the known universe, nothing registers on his scans. The vessel has catapulted beyond the reach of starlight by at least a hundred trillion light-years. Then a planetary-mass object materializes behind them. It's burning brightly even without a star to heat it. Hundreds of damaged ships are locked in its orbit. The crew discovers there are no life-signs aboard any of them. As system failures sweep through the Hummel, neither Chalmers nor the pilot can prevent the vessel from crashing into the surface near a mysterious ancient city. And that's where the real nightmare begins.

LUNA
by Rick Chesler

On the threshold of opening the moon to tourist excursions, a private space firm owned by a visionary billionaire takes a team of non-astronauts to the lunar surface. To address concerns that the moon's barren rock may not hold long-term allure for an uber-wealthy clientele, the company's charismatic owner reveals to the group the ultimate discovery: life on the moon.

But what is initially a triumphant and world-changing moment soon gives way to unrelenting terror as the team experiences firsthand that despite their technological prowess, the moon still holds many secrets.

CHECK OUT OTHER GREAT
SCIENCE FICTION BOOKS

IN PERPETUITY
by Jake Bible

For two thousand years, Earth and her many colonies across the galaxy have fought against the Estelian menace. Having faced overwhelming losses, the CSC has instituted the largest military draft ever, conscripting millions into the battle against the aliens. Major Bartram North has been tasked with the unenviable task of coordinating the military education of hundreds of thousands of recruits and turning them into troops ready to fight and die for the cause.

As Major North struggles to maintain a training pace that the CSC insists upon, he realizes something isn't right on the Perpetuity. But before he can investigate, the station dissolves into madness brought on by the physical booster known as pharma. Unfortunately for Major North, that is not the only nightmare he faces- an armada of Estelian warships is on the edge of the solar system and headed right for Earth!

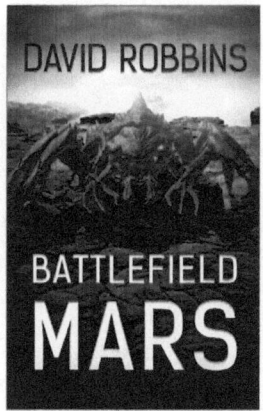

BATTLEFIELD MARS
by David Robbins

Several centuries into the future, Earth has established three colonies on Mars. No indigenous life has been discovered, and humankind looks forward to making the Red Planet their own.

Then 'something' emerges out of a long-extinct volcano and doesn't like what the humans are doing.

Captain Archard Rahn, United Nations Interplanetary Corps, tries to stem the rising tide of slaughter. But the Martians are more than they seem, and it isn't long before Mars erupts in all-out war.

CHECK OUT OTHER GREAT SCIENCE FICTION BOOKS

MAUSOLEUM 2069
by **Rick Jones**

Political dignitaries including the President of the Federation gather for a ceremony onboard Mausoleum 2069. But when a cloud of interstellar dust passes through the galaxy and eclipses Earth, the tenants within the walls of Mausoleum 2069 are reborn and the undead begin to rise. As the struggle between life and death onboard the mausoleum develops, Eriq Wyman, a one-time member of a Special ops team called the Force Elite, is given the task to lead the President to the safety of Earth. But is Earth like Mausoleum 2069? A landscape of the living dead? Has the war of the Apocalypse finally begun? With so many questions there is only one certainty: in space there is nowhere to run and nowhere to hide.

RED CARBON
by D.J. Goodman

Diamonds have been discovered on Mars.

After years of neglect to space programs around the world, a ruthless corporation has made it to the Red Planet first, establishing their own mining operation with its own rules and laws, its own class system, and little oversight from Earth. Conditions are harsh, but its people have learned how to make the Martian colony home.

But something has gone catastrophically wrong on Earth. As the colony leaders try to cover it up, hacker Leah Hartnup is getting suspicious. Her boundless curiosity will lead her to a horrifying truth: they are cut off, possibly forever. There are no more supplies coming. There will be no more support. There is no more mission to accomplish. All that's left is one goal: survival.

CHECK OUT OTHER GREAT SCIENCE FICTION BOOKS

SALVAGE MERC ONE
by Jake Bible

Joseph Laribeau was born to be a Marine in the Galactic Fleet. He was born to fight the alien enemies known as the Skrang Alliance and travel the galaxy doing his duty as a Marine Sergeant. But when the War ended and Joe found himself medically discharged, the best job ever was over and he never thought he'd find his way again.

Then a beautiful alien walked into his life and offered him a chance at something even greater than the Fleet, a chance to serve with the Salvage Merc Corp.

Now known as Salvage Merc One Eighty-Four, Joe Laribeau is given the ultimate assignment by the SMC bosses. To his surprise it is neither a military nor a corporate salvage. Rather, Joe has to risk his life for one of his own. He has to find and bring back the legend that started the Corp.

SERENGETI
by J.B. Rockwell

It was supposed to be an easy job: find the Dark Star Revolution Starships, destroy them, and go home. But a booby-trapped vessel decimates the Meridian Alliance fleet, leaving Serengeti—a Valkyrie class warship with a sentient AI brain—on her own; wrecked and abandoned in an empty expanse of space. On the edge of total failure, Serengeti thinks only of her crew. She herds the survivors into a lifeboat, intending to sling them into space. But the escape pod sticks in her belly, locking the cryogenically frozen crew inside.

Then a scavenger ship arrives to pick Serengeti's bones clean. Her engines dead, her guns long silenced, Serengeti and her last two robots must find a way to fight the scavengers off and save the crew trapped inside her.